For days now, Eden had been resisting LJ's spell, though she was glad her son had no such agenda.

As LJ quieted her boy, Eden's toes curled and tingles raced along her skin.

Liam won't remember this. But I'll never be able to forget.

Once they were home, she did not want to sit in her rocking chair late at night and wonder if she'd made the right choices—not about bringing Liam into the world, but about her own resistance in giving him a father.

Watching LJ with Liam rocked her confidence. Watching LJ made her *want*.

Father and son…

Man-woman-child…

Man and woman…

With LJ involved, any and all of those combinations seemed like the golden ticket.…

Dear Reader,

Family. Quirky, loyal, maddening, inspiring—it's the bedrock of our lives. What I like best about family is that it can be created in so many ways. Through birth and adoption, marriage and friendships that deepen into something lifelong, we create our kin. Then we jump on the roller coaster, and whether we're shrieking with laughter or shaking through breath-stealing drops, it helps to know we're hanging on together.

I'm thrilled to be part of LOGAN'S LEGACY REVISITED. Those Logan boys aren't perfect, but when they each meet the woman they can't resist, they step up to the plate…eventually. LJ Logan's life plan doesn't include baby spit up, diaper wipes or even a wife. Then he meets Eden. Strong as steel, soft as butter, she and her baby boy make mincemeat of LJ's master plan. I hope you enjoy their roller-coaster ride to happily ever after. Don't forget the Dramamine.

All the best,

Wendy Warren

THE BABY BARGAIN

WENDY WARREN

SPECIAL EDITION

Published by Silhouette Books

America's Publisher of Contemporary Romance

Special thanks and acknowledgment are given
to Wendy Warren for her contribution to the
LOGAN'S LEGACY REVISITED miniseries.

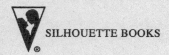 SILHOUETTE BOOKS

ISBN-13: 978-0-373-28068-1
ISBN-10:   0-373-28068-8

THE BABY BARGAIN

Copyright © 2007 by Harlequin Books S.A.

Visit Silhouette Books at www.eHarlequin.com

Printed in U.S.A.

WENDY WARREN

lives with her husband Tim, a dog, a cat and their recent—and most exciting!—addition, baby daughter Elisabeth near the Pacific Northwest's beautiful Willamette River. Their house was previously owned by a woman named Cinderella, who bequeathed them a garden full of flowers they try desperately (and occasionally successfully) not to kill, and a pink General Electric oven, circa 1958, that makes the kitchen look like an *I Love Lucy* rerun.

A two-time recipient of Romance Writers of America's RITA® Award for Best Traditional Romance, Wendy loves to read and write the kind of books that remind her of the old movies she grew up watching with her mom—stories about decent people looking for the love that can make an ordinary life heroic. Wendy was an *Affaire de Coeur* finalist for Best Up and Coming Romance Author of 1997. When not writing, she likes to take long walks, settle in for cozy chats with good friends and sneak tofu into her husband's dinner. She always enjoys hearing from readers and may be reached at P.O. Box 1208 Ashland, OR 97520.

For Tim Blough,
Libbi's first hero. And my last.
Thank you for filling our lives with laughter,
integrity and love. Every heroine should be so lucky.

Chapter One

It was going well.

Lawrence Logan, Jr., LJ to his family and friends, stood in the pastel-toned meeting room of the Children's Connection and managed, despite the overly cozy decor, to deliver a presentation guaranteed to knock the socks off the fertility and adoption clinic's board members and staff. He was about to save the Portland, Oregon business from going down in flames after a series of tough breaks and terrible publicity.

It felt good to be a savior.

"The Children's Connection has taken hits

on local news and in print. That can't be denied," he told his listeners in a smooth, authoritative voice that was neither judgmental nor commiserating.

"Fortunately for us, there are more viewers watching *American Idol* than the local news at six. Via high-visibility commercial spots, a redesigned Web site and strategic interviews, we will redirect general awareness and reprogram public opinion. It can be done, ladies and gentlemen. Logan Public Relations is going to show you how." Like a proud coach, he smiled at everyone around the table. "Let me give you a taste of what we have in mind."

Taking two steps to a TV monitor, he prepared to start the video presentation he'd brought with him.

Behind him, chairs creaked as people angled for a better view. LJ's adrenaline surged.

As a New York public relations consultant who was good at his job—in the interest of full disclosure make that *great* at his job—LJ was used to winning his clients' trust and, eventually, their gratitude. He enjoyed the expressions of satisfaction and relief that relaxed their strained features when he presented a watertight plan to give their floundering businesses the spit-polished patina of success.

A new job was always a rush, but this one was different. This job promised less work but higher stakes. Winning this client's trust was critical to a bigger game plan. If—no, *when*—LJ successfully bolstered the Children's Connection's flagging public image, he would be saving more than a business: he'd be saving a family…his own.

Not a bad day's work for a thirty-seven-year-old man who considered himself something of a black sheep.

Adjusting a silk tie that was bloody uncomfortable, but worth the bother because of the taste and affluence it projected, he glanced at the people watching the ten-minute-long DVD.

His uncle's family on his father's side had founded and now ran the Children's Connection. They'd been visibly stressed since he'd arrived in town. Past rumors of a black-market baby ring, insemination using the wrong donor sperm, kidnappings, and most recently the resignation of Robbie Logan, director of the day care center, had hammered the business like an Oregon storm.

Now the board of directors, including his uncle Terrence and aunt Leslie, plus assorted employees, including his cousin Jillian, watched the video. It offered mock-ups of two separate one-minute commercial campaigns, shot specifically for the Children's Connection, and LJ saw his aunt and uncle glance at each other in pleased surprise. Satisfaction stirred in his chest.

As the first commercial ended, the door to the meeting room clicked open…though not on the first try.

LJ couldn't help but watch as a medium-height, lavishly curved blonde juggled a plate and the largest water bottle he'd ever seen. As the only occupant of the room facing the blonde's direction, he was also the only person present to witness her difficulty in getting a good grip on the door handle. He took a step away from the TV monitor, intending to walk to the rear of the room and hold the door for her, but she solved her own problem by sticking the water bottle between her knees, holding the plate in one hand, widely opening the door with the other, then snatching the water bottle from between her knees and racing in.

Several people heard her that time and turned to acknowledge her entrance. She smiled and offered a brief wave of the water bottle.

Stationing herself near the door, a solitary figure behind the board members and coworkers who'd arrived on time and were seated in a U configuration around the conference tables, she proved taller than LJ had first thought and stronger looking, too. He'd dimmed the lights for the video viewing, but could see clearly that the arms she bared in a sleeveless robin's-egg-blue sweater bore no resemblance to the willowy, verging-on-emaciated model's limbs he'd grown used to after years in New York. The woman at the door looked like a farm girl, healthy and rosy, teeming with life.

She scanned the room for a vacant seat, but before she moved to the table, the TV monitor caught her attention. Eyes bigger and softer than Bambi's focused on the screen. Her full lips pursed in concentration. Everything about the woman—especially those lush lips—made LJ hunger to taste her....

Whoa. Time for an intervention.

LJ shook his head a bit. He'd never been one to lose track of the matter at hand and he didn't intend to start now.

Commanding himself to rise above the distraction, he refocused on the monitor, but admitted that the blonde's presence amplified the anticipation rushing through his veins.

On-screen, a woman twirled a toddler in a dandelion-carpeted field. Carefully filtered lighting softened all harsh lines and strong colors. A soothing voice-over scored the shot:

"The Children's Connection of Portland. Helping singles become families." Music swelled. The mother pulled her toddler close, and they both tumbled, laughing, into the grass. "Pursue your dream."

LJ nodded imperceptibly. After the commercial the video continued with statistics, demographics. LJ knew, though, that he'd hooked his audience already. No parent with a soul could fail to be moved. Hell, even he felt a little teary, and he was about as paternal as Scrooge.

Without question, single women eager to have babies would consider the Children's Connection again as their first choice in fertility clinics. Though the commercial they'd just viewed was a mock-up, once it was shot at budget and aired repeatedly, it would seep into viewers' hearts like honey into warm bread. LJ had to force himself not to turn toward the blonde to savor her reaction along with the others'. He written this spot himself.

There were times, like now, when he knew exactly what he was doing with his life.

Gag. Me.

That was Eden Carter's first reaction as she stood in the back of the meeting room and tried not to laugh out loud.

Only a man could possibly have come up with the pablum they'd just watched. More specifically, the man would have to be child-less or someone who had never asked his wife a single purposeful question about her mothering experience.

The Barbie doll in the commercial looked as if she'd never missed a night's sleep, for crying out loud. Her face was gorgeous, her figure toned and perfect, her hair an überstylist's work of art.

Come to the Children's Connection, Eden thought, *we'll help you have a baby who hardly ever cries and will never bite your boob while he's nursing.*

Okay, so maybe she was cranky, but she'd missed lots of sleep lately. Whoever had written the syrupy commercial should have asked her—or any of the single mothers who had been helped by the Children's Connection—what parenting an infant or toddler on one's own really looked like.

Shifting the arm that held the plate of cookies she'd brought to the meeting, she surreptitiously pressed her forearm against her right breast with its poor aching nipple.

Her beautiful baby boy, Liam, was currently adding a new tooth to the three he already had. He'd clamped down on her right nipple so hard this morning that she'd let out a shriek before she could stop herself. Her poor little guy had opened his blue eyes wide then started to squall. It had been a rough finish to a morning that had started late because she'd been up half the night applying a homeopathic teething gel to his swollen gums.

Liam wasn't the only one who depended on her availability day and night. As a doula, she was responsible for her patients anytime they needed her.

If she tried to twirl in a field like the gal in the commercial, she'd collapse from exhaustion.

Women who wanted to become parents, especially single parents, needed the kind of support and compassion that came from shared experience, and *truth*, not something so…so…

Silly!

When several people whipped around in their chairs to face her, she realized she'd spoken aloud.

"Do you want to comment, Eden?" Terrence Logan asked her with interest.

In her teens and early twenties, she'd had a bothersome tendency to speak first and think later. A committed yoga and meditation practice had soothed her jangled spirit and given her the discipline to insert a little lag time between her thoughts and her words.

Evidently she was suffering a relapse.

"No, thank you. Very sorry," she said since she'd clearly spoken out of turn.

Her coworkers here knew her as the centered, hard-to-ruffle woman she'd become. She'd even Hypno-Birthed her way through an eighteen-hour delivery, thank you very much.

No one here was familiar with the Eden Carter who'd struggled through each painful day of her youth like a salmon slogging upstream. Back then her burdens had seemed to weigh more than she did, and sometimes she'd release her frustration by picking fights that weren't even hers.

Involuntarily her gaze met the speaker's. What was his name? He was one of the Logans, but belonged to a branch of the family that didn't have much to do with the Children's Connection, as far as she knew.

His articulate brows had hiked to express surprise then lowered quickly to a frown. At first glance he appeared almost confused, but as Eden watched he gathered his wits and smiled tightly, gearing up for a fight if necessary.

An answering thrill of anticipation shot through her, catching her off guard. She willed the feeling to pass and to leave in its stead a healing serenity.

"I'm sure we're all interested in what you have to say, Ms.…?"

Oh, geez. Move on, buddy. Please, move on. "Carter," she muttered.

"Ms. Carter." Silencing the monitor that had gone to blue screen, he flicked on the overhead lights and turned toward her again. "I realize you weren't here for the *entire* presentation, but you've obviously had a strong reaction to what you did see."

Eden's eyes narrowed to mirror his. The gauntlet had been tossed. Challenge vibrated beneath the committed politeness of his words. He'd invited her comments and undermined them in a single breath.

"There's a seat at the head of the table." He gestured with an innocence that would melt butter, but she understood that his intention was to put her on the spot. "Of course, you're welcome to stand if you prefer." He stepped to the side, indicating he was just as pleased as could be to give her the floor.

Eden smiled, as innocently as he. *You don't scare me, bub. I went through back labor.*

Adopting her smoothest gliding walk, she approached the front of the room, plate of cookies and water bottle in hand, and never broke eye contact with him.

As she drew near, she saw that his eyes were blue and that he was older than he'd seemed from across the room. On a bet, she'd risk good money that he was mid- to late thirties, at least. Her initial impression had been that he was the born-with-a-silver-spoon type, but the closer she got the less untouched by life he seemed.

She stood no more than a foot away when she noted the tension around his eyes, eyes that were almost as blue as hers and her son's. He shared her son's dark hair, too, though his was a smidge darker.

"Thank you," she said when he held out a chair. He waited until she was comfortably seated before assuming the seat next to her.

He smelled good. Cleaner and subtler than cologne, more delicious than plain soap. Seemed as though she rarely had an occasion to smell anything more interesting than baby powder lately, so his scent hit her twice as hard.

Buck up, Eden, she told herself. *You probably smell like baby spit up, which is why you have a point to make.*

With a big smile, she plopped her plate of

cookies atop the cleaned-for-company conference table and whipped off the crinkled foil cover.

"Chocolate chocolate chip and oatmeal butterscotch," she announced. "Help yourselves. Three points each if you're doing Weight Watchers."

Her coworkers gazed hungrily at her homemade treats. She saw Jillian Logan glance at Dianna March, who was on the board of directors. Ordinarily the board and the staff rarely attended the same meetings. When the staff alone gathered in the afternoon, juice and coffee flowed and there was no shortage of snacks, making the furniture before them look like a picnic table.

Formality and professionalism seemed to be the order of this afternoon, however.

The meeting room appeared more official, less warm and friendly. A carafe of water and a coffee urn sat atop a sideboard, with a small container of sugar and packets of artificial sweetener as the only nod to the afternoon energy slump. Her cookies, which normally would have been half-gone in the time it took for her to notice the difference in the room, sat untouched as everyone waited to see what the board members were going to do.

That's the problem, she thought. *We can't stop being ourselves just because we're in trouble.* That's what this place was about: family first. Real life first. That was one reason she loved it so: you didn't have to fake it to make it at the Children's Connection.

Contrarily, the commercial she'd just watched looked like a trailer for *The Sound of Music.*

"Afternoon, everyone." She raised a hand companionably. "I apologize for walking in late. I hope the cookies'll make up for it. I stopped by the baby center to check on Liam. He's been teething, and you know how that goes. Sleepless nights, cranky days and a nose like a lazy river—nothing ever comes of it, but it doesn't stop running. You just can't pay a child-care provider enough to deal with that, can you?"

Understanding smiles popped up around the room as heads bobbed. There, that was better. Dianna and fellow board member Wayne Thorpe looked almost human again. No matter what trouble they'd suffered recently, the Children's Connection wasn't all about business. That was one reason she'd moved clear from Kentucky to Oregon to take this job. She hoped to heaven this place would hang on to its unique character in the face of its struggles. It was so easy to forget who you were when you were scared.

Eden turned toward the man beside her. "Do you have children, Mr.…"

She cocked a brow even though she knew his last name was Logan. Same as the uncle and cousins who'd hired him. Still, it never hurt to let one's adversary believe he hadn't been worthy of much interest up to now.

To his credit, his surprise showed only in his eyes.

"Logan," he supplied. "And, no, I do not have children."

Eden nodded and made a mental note. A very crisp "No, I do not" rather than "Not yet" or "I haven't been so fortunate." She colored her responding "Ahh" with gentle implication.

"Your commercial was lovely to look at," she said sincerely. "Almost made me want to get pregnant again. *If* someone could guarantee I'd be like the woman in your ad. Now, there's a gal who looks as if she could have triplets and not lose any beauty sleep. Most of us moms with little ones are lucky if we brush our teeth before noon."

From her peripheral vision, Eden saw the women in the room nod and smile.

"I hope I'm not being too personal, Ms. Carter," LJ said, obviously realizing he could lose the ground he'd already gained if he wasn't careful, "but you're far more attractive than the actress who was hired for the commercial. If you have a child young enough to be teething, I think we put the wrong woman on TV."

Garnet Kearn beamed at him. Wayne Thorpe and Miles Remington raised their brows as if it was an option worth considering.

Score: Logan, 1. Carter, 0.

Eden couldn't ignore the fact that he'd just made her look like Gladys Kravitz, butting in where she didn't belong. When she'd first received the memo regarding the meeting, she'd considered the invitation to be little more than a courtesy. Who needed a layperson's input with an advertising pro onboard? Now that she'd met the whiz kid, she revised her opinion.

You need me, buddy boy. And I need you to protect my place of employment. She was determined to speak up whether he liked it or not.

Smiling as if she thought he'd paid her a compliment, Eden cracked her knuckles under the table. He might know advertising, but Mr. New York was about to discover that mommies and babies were *her* areas of expertise.

LJ relished the victory he'd just won. Before Ms. Carter had tossed in her two cents, he'd been about to tie this job into a bow pretty enough to impress his uncle. No way would he allow someone to undermine a victory that was only moments away.

Her gripe could waste a lot of time if the board wasn't savvy about marketing. No one on any sofa in any home in America had ever bought a product or service because it promised to make him look and feel exactly the way he looked and felt sitting in front of his TV.

Advertising, even for services like those provided by the Children's Connection, appealed to people's fantasies, to their idealized versions of themselves and the lives they would like to lead. Who fantasized about being overworked, sleep deprived and covered in baby puke?

He decided to use her objection to hammer his point home. *My apologies, beauty, but this is a business meeting, not Mommy and Me.*

"I'm glad you found the commercial aesthetically pleasing." He spoke directly to her. "We want to plant a strong, positive image in the mind of anyone looking into an adoption or fertility clinic."

When her pale brows gathered and it appeared she was going to rebut, he held the floor tenaciously, shifting his attention to the others.

"It goes without saying that the Children's Connection has suffered a number of blows to its image and that the result has been public questioning of the organization's agenda. More crucially, this board's basic values have come under attack. I intend to plant an image firmly in the minds of every viewer that leaves no doubt about the Children's Connection's first love—the creation of families. I want hopeful parents to know we are unabashedly romantic about helping to build those families and watching them grow. That we will be part of their lives far past inception or birth or an adoptive placement. The world may be cynical…the Portland Children's Connection is not."

LJ always knew when he'd hooked his audience. The energy in a conference room began to hum. If *he* felt it, he was making his point.

Around the table members of the board sat taller in their faux-leather chairs. LJ's uncle Terrence and aunt Leslie linked hands atop the table. The unconsciousness of the gesture told LJ a great deal.

Though he kept his gaze on the others, he could feel the frustration simmering in the woman seated beside him. What was her beef? So the actress in the commercial was skinny. Eden Carter's body was made to attract men, most of whom would go nuts over her more liberal curves. The subtle Southern lilt in her voice wouldn't hurt, either.

He had a fleeting desire to apologize for cutting off her protest—very fleeting. He'd never been that nice in business. And since he was about to win his father's approval for the first time in two decades, he wasn't about to let a pretty blonde with a body-image issue compete with his father-approval issue.

Beside him, the woman cleared her throat. When LJ looked at her, she smiled.

"That is a wonderful saying. 'The world may be cynical. The Children's Connection is not.'" She splayed a hand on her chest. "I'm a sucker for great sayings. I still get weepy over 'You had me at hello.' Still, if I understand the recent allegations, it's our credibility that's at question. We're being called irresponsible. Or out-and-out liars."

Damage control alert. LJ's brow furrowed so deeply he could have grown carrots. Eden Carter looked and sounded like an angel, but as she turned to address the people around the table, she was far from heavenly. She was a bad-ass thorn in his side.

As she began speaking, he ground his teeth and felt pain stab his head. If she gave him a migraine, he was going to stop being polite.

"In our First-Time Moms class we tell women exactly what to expect," she said in that soothing, eminently reasonable tone she had. "We insist they be armed with real-life information so their experience won't overwhelm their expectations. The public should know *that*. They should know we educate and arm our clients with knowledge before they become parents and while they're pregnant and after their babies arrive. Our prospective clients and all those nasty people who have been so rude to us need to know we would never ever try to snow anyone. We don't merely *value* honesty around here, we insist on it."

She thumped, actually thumped a fist on the table. He almost felt sorry for her, because she'd obviously forgotten that she was addressing a board of directors, not just a roomful of fellow employees. If this were a Frank Capra movie and Jimmy Stewart were on the board, fist-thumping idealism *might* work.

"If our intentions are in question," she continued, as earnest as could be, "then, shouldn't we be as frank as possible now? We don't have to sugarcoat reality to make it palatable. The truth is good enough. The Children's Connection is good enough." She placed both palms on the table and sat forward in her chair. "I ought to know. I work here, *and* I'm a client."

Hold the phone.

LJ's brain, which was starting to hurt, scrambled to take in the information that she was a Children's Connection *client.* By God, he loathed surprises.

How was she a client? Of which services had she availed herself? Adoption or the fertility clinic?

And what did she do here, anyway?

Racking his brain some more, he sought a polite way to remind everyone present that he was the professional here and that Little Bo Peep didn't know advertising from a flock of sheep.

He opened his mouth, but applause came out. Huh? Frowning, he glanced around.

Every soul around the table had his or her hands in prayer position, clapping enthusiastically. Heads nodded. Broad, unmistakably proud smiles wreathed every face.

He looked to his left.

Eden Carter ducked her head humbly, adding an "Oh, pshaw" shrug before she picked up her plate of cookies and passed it around.

And he was worried about finding a polite way to discredit her?

His irritation rose and his head pounded harder with each "Ahhh" a bite of her apparently excellent baked goods inspired.

The hell with polite.

The meeting was out of his control, the first time he recalled that happening *ever,* and he had five feet, six inches of curving Betty Crocker to thank for it.

When the plate of cookies made it back to their end of the table, she reached in front of him and held it aloft. Unshakably pleasant, she offered, "Cookie? Only—"

"Three Weight Watchers points?" he recited along with her. "I heard." Smiling with no humor at all, he reached for a perfectly round disk studded with chocolate chips. Examined it. "It looks good. And sweet."

Returning the cookie to the plate, he curled his lips into something feral. "But I'm an Atkins man." He leaned toward her, his words for her ears only. "See, I have a goal. Don't think for one second that I'm going to let a little sugar get in my way."

Chapter Two

"Then he looked at me with his beady eyes all scrunched up and nasty and said, 'Don't think for one second I'm going to be nice about this!' Or something like that. That was the idea, anyway."

Eden sat on an Elmo beach towel spread atop the grass in Woodstock Park and recounted the afternoon's weirdness for her best friend and housemate, Liberty Sanchez. Eden's accent, modulated and subtle on a typical day, sounded particularly twangy when anger became her overriding emotion. "Oh, mah Gaawwwwd, what a weasel."

Snatching a red grape from the bag she'd brought for their dinner picnic and popping it into her mouth, Liberty shrugged with the fatalism she'd developed over her thirty years. "Sounds like a typical businessman. You get in his way, you're dust." Her near-black eyes narrowed. "Was it so important to make your point, Eden? I mean, I know you care about your business, but as long as what's-his-face—"

"Lawrence Logan, Jr., rich boy."

"As long as Junior saves the day, does it matter so much how he does it?"

Eden cast her friend a look of disbelief. "Since when did you decide the end justifies the means? I do like that you called him Junior, though."

Remaining worked up, she slapped her hand on the towel, close to her playing son, who dropped his Elmo phone. Swiftly, Eden retrieved the toy and handed it back. "Sorry, honey. Mommy is in a snit, all right. You gotta bear with me. Some people get under my skin, and I just can't scratch hard enough."

"Maybe," Liberty said with her usual dry brand of calm, "the problem is you scratch yourself and think the other person is going to bleed."

Eden scowled at her best friend since middle school. "You have got to stop going to those twelve-step groups. You're absolutely ruining my resentments."

Liberty said nothing more. Wrapping up the grapes and stashing them in a plastic container along with a tofu quiche she'd made for their dinner, she stowed the container in a nylon backpack and slipped the straps over her shoulders. While Eden got Liam ready for the short walk home, Liberty shook out their blanket.

Watching her friend, Eden knew, as she'd always known, that although she and Liberty had reacted differently to their life circumstances, they'd both grown a protective armor that functioned as a second skin. Most of the time they understood each other quite well. They were excellent roommates and good friends. Moreover, Liberty was studying at night to be an ob-gyn nurse. Eden had wondered whether introducing a baby to the mélange would encourage Liberty to look elsewhere for housing, but her roommate's enjoyment of babies had smoothed the path so far.

Fitting Liam into his front carrier became easier with an extra set of hands as Liberty wordlessly adjusted the straps Eden had trouble reaching.

"Thanks." She passed Liberty the Elmo phone and took the cold purple teething ring Liberty handed her. Liam accepted it eagerly from his mother and began gumming. "You always know just what he needs. You sure you don't want one of these? I know a great fertility clinic."

Liberty's laugh sounded like a squawk. "No, thank you." She smoothed Liam's dark baby curls. "I'll stick to helping them come into the world and babysitting this one."

It was the answer Eden expected. Liberty's childhood had been as tough as Eden's, one reason they'd bonded as girls and remained tight as they sprinted toward thirty. Whereas Liberty had decided she didn't know enough about happy families to help create one, Eden for years had longed to start a family of her own and to give her kids what she had not had—a magical childhood.

Like Liberty, she enjoyed the work of bringing children into the world. That, coupled with her keen interest in natural medicine, had led to her work as a doula and eventually to her job at the Children's Connection. She'd worked hard, made a nice home, but had never met *the* guy. It wasn't as if she hadn't tried. Just the opposite: she'd tried too hard.

The fallout from her failed relationships polluted the memory of her late teens and early twenties. Truth be told, she'd had a few too many relationships.

Her head had been so doggone stuffed with dreams about forever and about that big strong somebody she could cling to in times of trouble...geez Louise, her poor brain hadn't had any room to work.

She'd turned a new leaf, thank God. Hadn't had a relationship in an age, and never let herself even think anymore about strong arms and a man who'd die for her and blah, blah, blah.

Her Southern ancestors may have thought it was impossible to raise a family without a man, but Eden knew better. It would have been pure foolishness to wait until she'd met someone marriageable before she'd had a baby. Her ovaries might have been the size of pinheads by then.

Besides, she'd learned the hard way that waiting for someone to fix things generally meant you stayed broken. A smart woman solved her own problems.

And a scared woman made deals with her Maker. Eden had made one.

Since the age of fourteen, she'd been keeping a journal in which she wrote down her thoughts about life, her hopes and prayers and gripes. A few years ago, when she'd decided to have a child on her own, she'd written it in her diary like this: "God, give me a baby, and you'll never have a single cause to call me an unmindful mother."

From the time she'd conceived, she'd known her first priority would always be Liam. Nothing would get in the way of providing a lighthearted and stable growing-up time for her little boy. And that meant—

NO MORE MEN.

She'd written that in her journal, too, with a red permanent marker. Her life had fallen apart when she was ten because of a man. She'd been in second grade when her mother, an artist with a wild spirit, had become a bit too wild. By the time her mother was diagnosed with manic depression, her stepfather had thrown in the towel on the marriage and their family. Her birth father was no help, having moved with no forwarding address before Eden learned to say "Dada." Two men had broken her heart and she'd spent the better part of her young womanhood acting as if a man was the glue to put it back together. It upset her to think about it, because she so, *so* knew better!

Now that she'd finally gotten her mind settled on being a singleton, it was just God's sense of humor to give her a case of hormones that made her libido jumpier than a frog on fire.

Pregnancy had increased her cravings for more than Doritos and peanut-butter-cup ice cream. Fortunately, she'd had work to focus on during the months she'd carried Liam. Then she'd given birth, and postpartum concerns trumped sexual interest any day of the week.

Drat LJ Logan for showing up and revving her engine even while he was busy irritating her. The man had some powerful phero-mones, and the truth was he'd been on her mind all evening.

"I wonder what Junior's story is," she murmured, knowing she should have bitten her tongue. It was just the simple truth that one of her failings as a human was her habit of thinking about the very things she shouldn't.

Liam dropped his teething ring. Liberty made a beautiful save and handed it back without missing a beat. "Story about what?" she asked.

"About why he doesn't want kids."

"How do you know that? From what you told me, the two of you didn't get chatty."

"Well, no, but I asked him straight out whether he had any. His answer was absolutely a negative. The boy practically shouted it."

"So you stayed after the meeting and talked to him?"

"I asked him during the meeting."

"In front of the board? In front of the people who hired him?"

"Of course, and don't look at me like that." Heat suffused Eden's face and chest. "I was trying to make a point."

"You're not supposed to make points in front of a man's boss. Not if you hope to have even a barely civil relationship with him."

"I don't need a civil relationship with LJ Logan." That was the truth, too. "I need him to do his job well enough to help save the Children's Connection, and right now I have my doubts."

Liberty shook her head. "As long as I've known you, you've had excellent interpersonal skills."

Eden was about to say thank you when her roommate added, "Except when it comes to men. Then you're a dolt."

Eden stopped walking. "I beg your pardon, please? I have *never* had complaints from males regarding my communication skills."

Liberty patted her shoulder. "Don't get your thong in a knot. You start to sound like Scarlett O'Hara when you're upset." She continued walking. "All I'm saying is, remember Hal Sneeden? He called you emotionally withholding."

Eden felt a stab of pain but told herself to ignore it. "Oh, that." She waved a hand and strolled after Liberty. "That doesn't mean I can't communicate. I never wanted to get emotionally intimate with Hal Sneeden. And you agreed I could never get serious about him, anyway. Remember? Because if we'd gotten married I'd have been Eden Sneeden."

Leaving the park, they headed down the sidewalk toward home. "People would have said, 'There go Eden Sneeden's kids.'" Bending forward, she kissed Liam's head. "I would never do that to you, precious."

Liberty's throaty laugh lightened the atmosphere, but inside Eden struggled not to feel hurt all over again. The breakup with Hal had happened seven years ago, and when she recalled his words they still gnawed at the edges of her confidence, like bugs on a leaf. His exact words had been, "I've never felt really close to you."

Well, shoot! She gritted her teeth as tears gathered at the corners of her eyes. She didn't care a fig about Hal Sneeden anymore; she really didn't. But even though she'd dated much more frequently than Liberty had, it had not escaped her notice that Liberty had close platonic relationships with men, whereas she, Eden, had never had a boyfriend she could also call her friend.

She chewed on that some as they walked the brief route home, where families—the typical, nuclear variety—dotted their path like land mines.

Passing a gray bungalow, both she and Liberty raised their hands to wave to the Scotts, a family of five that included three kids, a mother and a father, all of whom could be found outside playing or working together on even the poorest excuse for a nice day. Farther ahead were the Michaelsons—two toddlers, working mom, stay-at-home dad who liked to construct temporary forts out of fallen branches and twigs. Like their neighbors, they were determinedly finding things to do outside, relishing the early spring weather before the next spate of April showers.

Outwardly, Eden kept smiling. Secretly she couldn't wait to get home, where she could hole up inside the rest of the night and ignore all the happy three-, four- and five-somes.

Portland was truly a family town. Several years back it had been touted as one of the ten best cities in the country in which to raise children. That made it a great place to pursue her work as a childbirth coach. A terrific place to have and raise Liam. It was less terrific when she didn't want to be reminded that Liam might someday think she'd short-changed him by bringing him into the world without a daddy.

And sometimes when she lay in bed—not at night, but in the morning—and listened to the twitter of birds and the sound of her son's breathing, she wished for someone to turn to, to whisper with, to plan the day.

She glanced down as Liam's head bobbed against her chest. The motion of walking lulled him into his evening snooze. Gently, she stroked the hair around his ears. *You're the only guy for me from now on, little man.* Still, it would be nice to be part of a larger community.

"I read about a woman in Florida who started a cooperative housing development," she said contemplatively to Liberty. "The intention is to bring foster kids together with people who want to adopt or at least mentor children. The housing is available to people of all ages. You can even eat together in a common dining hall."

Liberty eyed her doubtfully. "It sounds like a dorm."

Eden laughed. "No, really, co-op communities sound like nice places. Most have common areas for the kids to play together. Some even do cooperative babysitting and there's a deliberate effort to make the communities multigenerational, which is great for the kids." She ran her fingers over Liam's soft dark curls, so different from her wavy blond hair. "It would be nice to think he's with people who feel like…"

"Like family without the need for therapeutic intervention?"

This time Eden's laughter rang out down the street. "You are such a cynic."

"Mmm."

They reached their block of smaller Portland-style bungalows, and Liberty stepped up her pace. "I've got major studying to do. I'm going to head to First Cup for something very tall, very strong and very iced. You want?"

"Nope." Eden hadn't done caffeine since the stick turned pink, and she didn't particularly need more calories tonight. She nodded to Liam. "If the master of the house sleeps a little longer, I just might look up the co-op projects in Portland."

"Have at it. Just don't expect me to move with you. I like my privacy."

Both women stopped talking when they reached their house. Parked in front was a sleek black Cadillac coupe. An impatient-looking man leaned indolently against the dry-rot-damaged porch rail Eden kept promising herself she would fix. Dark glasses hid his eyes.

"Speaking of tall and strong," Liberty murmured.

Eden shook her head. What was *he* doing here? She stared at LJ Logan, only assuming he stared back from behind the expensive-looking shades.

"You left out *icy*," she said.

"What?" Liberty gazed toward the porch unabashedly. By choice, she didn't date, but she wasn't shy.

"*That's* LJ Logan." Eden spoke out the side of her mouth, keeping her voice low. "Very tall, probably strong, and could freeze water with his tongue."

"That's the guy you tangled with?"

"Yeah."

Liberty gave an exaggerated wag of her dark head. *"El es muy guapo."*

"Cut it out," Eden whispered, trying not to move her lips. "For all we know he speaks Spanish."

"Ooh. Then he might—just might—be worth dating."

Ignoring her roommate, Eden slowly approached her porch, curious but warier than a cat in a dog run. Portland General Hospital, which housed the Children's Connection, was located across the river, at least thirty to forty minutes from her neighborhood if there was any traffic at all.

"You're a long way from the west side," she said to LJ when she was close enough to speak softly over Liam's head and still be heard.

"Ain't it the truth?" A smile spread slowly across LJ's face, softening the bored rich-man expression. He nodded at Liberty. "Evening. I see you've been enjoying the good weather." Still without moving off the porch or even uncrossing his arms, he focused on the baby sleeping against Eden's chest. "And this must be the teether you mentioned. He looks happy now."

Liberty joined Eden, standing near her shoulder. "He doesn't seem icy," she cracked sotto voce. More loudly, she said, "Well, we've just come back from a picnic. I've got to put the leftovers in the fridge."

Jogging lightly up the steps, she stopped alongside LJ, who straightened away from the porch rail and extended his hand.

"LJ Logan," he said, by way of introduction, "one of Ms. Carter's coworkers. And you are?"

"Libertad Sanchez." Liberty laid on the Spanish accent, which she could turn on and off as easily as she worked a faucet. "Roommate," she added. "Also in-house natural foods chef and the voice of Eden's conscience. I have a fruit-sweetened berry crisp in the kitchen, and you're welcome to try it as long as you didn't come here to rake Eden over the coals. She already feels *terrible* for dissing you in your business meeting."

"Liberty!"

Without a glance at Eden, Liberty gave LJ a sexy smile and a shrug. "I tried. You two play nice. Try to set a good example for the baby."

She disappeared into the house. More slowly than her friend, Eden walked up the steps. She looked Mr. Logan straight in the sunglasses.

"I did not 'dis' you. I stated my opinion calmly and courteously."

He cocked his head. "Where are you from?"

"Pardon me?"

"I'm trying to place your accent. It comes and goes. Right now it's a little thick, so I'm guessing that you've worked hard to eradicate it, but when you're tense it comes back."

Eden, who liked to think she had total control over the accent she had indeed tried to eradicate, frowned at him unhappily. "Mr. Logan, it's after work hours and you haven't told me why you are here."

He nodded. "You see? You said, *heah.* You're stressed around me. Like you were at the meeting. Why was that?"

He was sure right about her being stressed now, Eden thought; he liked to knock her off track. The conversation kept changing direction, and still he hadn't answered her question. "Why are you—" she stopped short of saying *heah* "—present?"

Teeth that had been straightened to perfection flashed in a grin. His entire being oozed male charm. "To be perfectly frank, I'm not certain why I'm here, Ms. Carter. Why don't you ask me in—or at least invite me to have a seat on your very inviting porch—and perhaps we'll both find out."

Eden gestured to the porch.

"You can sit there—" she nodded toward a wicker chair with a tall fan back "—while I put the baby down."

Liam was asleep in his crib, changed and dressed in footed pajamas before she joined her self-invited guest. Garage-sale furniture, Goodwill crockery and a selection of organic herbs she kept watered and well-groomed decorated the porch he'd called inviting. She set a tray with two glasses of iced tea on a large wooden end table.

Settling into his chair's mate and wishing she'd had time to sand and paint her porch furniture in the last year, Eden watched LJ sip the herbal tea.

"It's…different. What is it?"

"Mostly fenugreek and blessed thistle, herbs that are good for lactating women. They increase milk supply."

He'd removed his sunglasses while she was in the house. The blue eyes she remembered from the meeting regarded her wryly. "And what, pray tell, will they do to me?"

Eden raised her glass. "Let's find out, shall we?" She drained half the glass, inviting him to do the same.

His appreciative laugh drew the glance of a neighbor walking his boxer. Eden waved.

"So we were going to figure out why I'm here," he said, making his own chair creak as he leaned back. "I think I know."

She waited while he let the suspense build. He was quite the politician, working his audience, watching for the reaction. Her continued silence didn't seem to bother him in the least.

"I like you," he said finally. "Your coworkers like you. I'd go so far as to say they respect your opinion. That says something."

"And did you charm one of my respectful coworkers into giving you my address?"

"Not at all. I charmed one of them into letting me look at the company files."

Surprised by his honesty, she let herself relax. "You're unrepentant."

"I'm determined. I'd like to talk to you about my plan for the Children's Connection campaign."

"Isn't it the same one you showed us in the meeting?" She covered her mouth. "I apologize. I didn't mean for that to sound rude. I just mean I already saw it, and I…"

"Don't like it. Right."

When her cheeks reddened, he nodded and set his glass on the table between them. "This is why I want to talk to you again. I like you. I don't want you to say something you'll feel awful about. You see, I have a theory. You don't like my ideas…yet. But you do like me. And right now you're thinking to yourself, 'Eden, just give the guy a chance.'" He leaned toward her, smiling. "Am I right or am I right?"

Chapter Three

Eden felt a little moustache of nervous perspiration break out above her upper lip. Damn, he was good. And, she had to admit that when he leaned forward like that, his gaze focused as if she were the only person in the world, it was easy to forget he was here for one reason and one reason only: to make his own life easier by persuading her to support him.

"Actually," she demurred, shooting him an apologetic look, "I feel bad any time I have to tell a potentially hurtful truth. Why, once, I saw a neighbor's big old tomcat chasing a sweet little marmalade tabby and it was not the first time, let me tell you. I marched right across the street and knocked on that neighbor's door and said, 'Ma'am, your tomcat is behaving like the neighborhood bully. You'd better put a stop to it at once or he won't have any friends at all.' I felt awful then, too, but it had to be said."

Finished, she sat back, a butter-wouldn't-melt-in-her-mouth smile on her face. To his credit, LJ's eyes sparked in appreciation. He nodded. "Well, it was just a theory." Speaking more sincerely, he said, "I'm a public relations and marketing expert, Eden. I know what I'm doing. I can put the Children's Connection back in the community's good graces. And I can do it quickly. But it's going to be more difficult if one of the organization's favorite employees bad-mouths my ideas."

Modest, too, she thought wryly. "I don't doubt you know more about ad campaigns and promotions than I do, Mr. Logan."

"LJ."

"But I know about prospective parents. I won't restate all my objections to your approach, except to say again, since you're here, that I don't think we can establish credibility by looking as if we don't understand or are afraid to acknowledge reality. By that, I mean the reality of our troubles at the Connection *and* the reality of being a parent. Especially a single parent."

"I see." He mulled her words over. When he spoke again, she had to admit he didn't sound defensive at all. "Putting aside the problems at the Children's Connection for a moment," he said, "let's talk about the second part of your objection. You think my commercial showed disregard for the rigors of parenting by making life seem good, enjoyable. Do you enjoy your life, Eden?"

"Of course I do. That's not the point."

"How long have you been a single parent?"

"As long as I've been a mother, Mr. Logan."

"LJ."

"And, I work with mothers-to-be every day. When I say they don't want to be fed a lot of hearts-and-flowers malarkey, I know what I'm talking about." Because that sounded harsh, she added, "If you don't mind my saying so."

"Not a bit." A beat passed. "Did you

become a single parent intentionally or did Liam's father leave?"

Eden simply stared at her visitor. She might live in the Northwest now, but she'd been born in the South, where that question would surely be considered too personal. "I'm terribly sorry, but that information is not your business, Mr. Logan—"

"LJ—"

"*Mr. Logan.* Because after all, I barely know you."

"Hmm. That's true." He let a frown crease his handsome face. "On the other hand, you thought you knew me well enough this afternoon to discredit my work." He tilted his head, thinking, then decided aloud, "Yep. I earned the right to at least one personal question."

He managed to engender a perfectly nasty coil of guilt that zinged through her middle.

She gave him the slit-eyed look that worked great on Liberty's cat when it looked as if it was going to jump onto the dining table, a place it had no business going. "I don't like the way you worked that out. This afternoon was not personal. *At all.* I know the needs of our clients, because I understand their concerns. I was speaking from that vantage point."

Uncrossing his considerably long legs, LJ Logan planted his expensively shod feet squarely on her porch and rested his elbows on his knees. "Want to know what my vantage point is? Are you interested in my motivation?"

His voice remained low and almost melodious, but challenge lit his blue eyes. He was intelligent, energetic. Opinionated. But perhaps not as arrogant as she'd believed earlier. Perhaps. As they locked gazes, she was fairly certain she saw a request in his eyes, rather than a demand.

"Yes, I'm interested in your motivation."

A flicker of surprise yielded to a smile. "I don't believe in resting on my laurels, Eden. I study the most current research in my field, and it tells me consumers—*people*—give their trust and their money to the businesses they believe will make them feel good. Doesn't matter what kind of business we're talking about. Everyone wants someone to make his or her choices, his or her life easier. Yes, the woman in the commercial looked happy, healthy—"

"With a great hairdresser."

"She looked good, because advertising works when it makes the consumer believe you have what they want."

"Studies tell you this?"

"Yes."

"Well, I don't know about your studies. I'm a doula. I coach women through labor and I run the new single moms' group at the Children's Connection. The women I work with are worried about fluctuating hormones and how to find trustworthy, affordable child care on a single person's income. They're mighty concerned about having to go back to work on four hours of sleep a night. Their challenges will not be appeased by a thirty-second sound bite, and I would hate to have them assume we don't understand their struggles. Or that we think their journeys will be smooth sailing once they choose our clinic. That's a lie."

The edge of LJ's smile twitched with the effort to maintain it. "I'm not suggesting we lie to anyone. But we're not going to draw new clients to the Children's Connection by enumerating all the gory details of parenthood."

The gory details?

Why hadn't the Logans hired someone who understood the desire for children? Someone who valued family? LJ's blood connection to the other Logans was not reason enough to put all their fates—those of their past, current and future clients, too—into his hands.

"I was drawn by the center's forthrightness," she told him. "Even forthrightness about the mistakes that have been made."

"Kidnappings? Mix-ups in the sperm bank? Rumors of a black-market baby ring?" Emphatically, he shook his head. "The public doesn't need to be reminded about those matters. They're thinking about them already. That's why I'm here—to make them think about something else."

"The Children's Connection took responsibility wherever they were culpable. The way to calm doubts is to address allegations, not gloss over them."

They both sat on the edge of their seats now leaning over their legs. Eden enjoyed the opportunity to say exactly what she thought to this supremely confident businessman. He didn't seem to mind mixing it up with her, either.

"Fine. I understand your point of view, Eden, but—and I don't mean this in a condescending way—you're an employee who uses the day care center. The need for additional comfort and positive imaging will be far greater for single women who come to the center to find…" He frowned, losing momentum as he searched for a word. "When they need, uhh…"

Eden frowned, not knowing at first what LJ was trying to say. "Single women who need…?" She shook her head.

And then she understood.

"Oh, my God. Sperm?" She started to smile. "Are you trying to say 'sperm'? 'A single woman who comes to the center to find a sperm donor'? It's okay. I know that word."

"Obviously." Handsomely flushing because *he* hadn't said it, LJ straightened then leaned back in the chair. "You won't tell me how long you've been single, you refuse to use my first name, but you can say 'sperm' three times in two sentences?"

Eden tilted her head, pondering the thought. "It is ironic, isn't it?" She picked up her glass and swirled the iced tea. "Then again, I do work in a clinic that offers alternative insemination. A man's contributions to the process isn't something we romanticize."

"That information should render every man in Portland impotent," he grumbled, crossing his legs. The action looked so self-protective Eden nearly spewed her sip of iced tea.

LJ watched her. The smile she'd withheld from him before emerged freely now as she laughed. Her impossibly thick hair brushed her shoulders. Everything about her was generous—eyes, nose, lips and shoulders as gorgeously round and curving as her bosom.

He certainly didn't consider himself old-fashioned, but he couldn't comfortably discuss sperm with a woman whose presence reminded him of sex every time he looked at her. So sue him.

Why was he here, anyway? He wasn't convincing her of a thing.

Mystified, he shook his head. It wasn't like him to chase after approval. And, really, he didn't need hers. It would make his job easier, yes, but he didn't need it. He should leave.

"What is it about you?"

She blinked the huge, heavily lashed blue

eyes he kept losing his way in. "What do you mean?"

"I want you to support my plan for the Children's Connection. I'm not sure why."

His candor threw her off, which afforded some satisfaction. His ego had taken a bruising with her.

After a pause during which her brows almost touched, she repeated the reason he'd offered earlier. "Because you like me."

"I guess I must," he murmured.

LJ had studied body language in his determination to be the best salesman of his business. A firm, well-grounded stance communicated confidence, strength and assurance. He never fidgeted. Except now.

Moving to the edge of his seat again, even though he'd just relaxed back, he searched her baby-blue eyes. "How long have you been single?" he asked quietly.

Her full lips parted. Her breath quickened. Just a bit, but he noticed.

"What does this have to do with business?"

"Absolutely nothing. How long?"

If she'd chosen not to answer, he wouldn't have been surprised. He was beyond pleased when she did.

"I've never been married, Mr. Logan."

"LJ," he corrected calmly. "Is your son— Liam, isn't it?" She nodded, still wary. "Is Liam's father involved in his life? Or are you truly flying solo?"

Her breath had been shallow. Now she released a long sigh. "I'm truly flying solo. But I knew I would be. I planned for it. When I say single parenthood is difficult, I'm not complaining. It's simply a fact."

"Why did you plan for it?" His frown moved from the inside out. "Did the father walk out while you were pregnant?" He'd never had children and never intended to. The thought that she'd been left high and dry by someone she'd trusted annoyed the hell out of him. He'd long ago given up unprotected sex. As he saw it, no one in any relationship should enjoy that privilege if he didn't plan to stick around for the consequences.

Her long hair swung as she shook her head. "Nobody walked out. I told you, I don't just work at the Children's Connection. I've used their services."

It took a moment to compute that properly. She'd already mentioned that she had Liam in the child care center. The Children's Connection also had an adoption division. But except for darker, curlier hair, the baby looked just like her. So that left—

Holy—

"It's impolite to look shocked when you realize someone has used a sperm bank," she reprimanded with that honeyed twang.

"Too bad. That's the only look I have at the moment."

Dimples appeared in her cheeks. "Honestly, I don't know whether to laugh or rap you on the knuckles. You are going to promote an agency that specializes in alternatives to traditional pregnancy. You cannot look shocked every time you meet one of our mothers."

"I won't look shocked *every* time. I'm shocked now because you're young. Not a victim of the biological clock. And you're objectively attractive to men. It's hard for me to believe you couldn't find someone with whom to start a family. And now I think you're blushing, but it's getting dark, so I can't quite tell."

She lowered her head, allowing her hair to fall into her face for a few moments before she raked it back with her fingers.

"Do you say everything that's on your mind?" she demanded.

"Of course not." He brushed aside the idea. "I'm in public relations. Discreet is my middle name. Do you know who your sperm donor was?"

"Mr. Logan!"

"LJ."

Eden *was* blushing, right down to her toes. She felt heat surging, well, pretty much everywhere.

Before she'd decided to pursue alternative insemination, she hadn't had a steady relationship in almost a year. She certainly hadn't had a relationship since, so that put her in the middle of a two-year dry spell.

The truth was she didn't miss any specific person with whom she'd been in involved. What she missed was the *idea* of someone, all the terrific fantasies she used to build up during the honeymoon phase.

But "forever" had remained for her nothing more than an increasingly uncomfortable yearning. Finally, she'd decided that the hunt for happily-ever-after was like looking for the lost city of Atlantis.

The truth was that she was better, calmer, steadier without all the drama.

As for sex, at first she'd only missed it every now and again.

Then she'd pursued alternative insemination and gotten pregnant with Liam, and her hormones had gone haywire. She'd experienced the normal rise in libido during pregnancy, with unfortunately no one to help her exercise it.

Mothers with partners complained all the time about lack of desire and about their significant others' frustration with a greatly reduced sex life.

In a seriously ironic twist, Eden found herself still highly charged after childbirth. Hormones. Couldn't live with them, couldn't live without them.

She was certain her hormones were at least partly responsible for the fact that she was attracted to LJ Logan.

True, he was handsome, had a sense of humor and a way of staring at her that made her skin feel hot and goose bumpy at the same time. But he was also impertinent, a little arrogant and very single-minded.

He really annoyed her.

When she wasn't completely turned on.

"Of course I know who the sperm donor was," she said, not sure why she'd decided to answer, except that she didn't want him to think that either she or the Children's Connection were irresponsible. "I chose him."

He pondered that awhile. "I want to know more. Like why you chose a donor instead of the real thing."

"I got the 'real thing,'" she countered. "Without unnecessary complications."

A smile eased across his face. "You consider sex an unnecessary complication?"

Yes. No. "I wasn't referring to sex."

He grinned. "Answer, anyway."

He was flirting with her, no question, but the flirtation was playful. Because her heart skipped several times, she answered honestly to eliminate any notion that she might be waiting for a man.

"Yes. Okay. Sex *is* a complication. Relationships in general are a complication."

If she was expecting an argument, she was mistaken.

He spread his arms in a gesture that said, "See? We agree."

He might have elaborated, but Liam didn't

give him the chance. The baby started bawling, the quality of the cry suggesting he'd had a bad dream or was wet. Eden jumped up. More slowly, LJ rose also.

They stared at each other, neither moving until Liam cried louder.

"I'd better go." This time they both spoke at once.

Eden did her best to ignore the foolish side of her that felt disappointed. Instead, she nodded. "Thank you for dropping by," she said perfunctorily, figuring that if he'd driven all the way out here to secure her support he was leaving disappointed, so she ought to at least be polite.

He opened the screen door for her, a chivalrous move that surprised her. She hadn't seen a man move that swiftly to open a door he didn't intend to walk through himself since she'd left Kentucky.

A hiccupping cry from her baby had her muttering, "Thanks," and heading inside, leaving LJ Logan to do…whatever LJ Logan did with his evenings.

"He's dry and doesn't want his teether. Must have had a bad dream, poor little guy." Cradling the baby, Liberty greeted Eden at the door to the bedroom Eden shared with her son.

She'd positioned the chair by a window to take advantage of silver moonlight when she nursed late at night and it seemed that she and Liam were the only people awake in the world.

"Do you want the Boppy?" Liberty asked. Eden nodded and Liberty placed a sturdy crescent-shaped pillow on her friend's lap.

Settling Liam atop the Boppy, Eden raised the T-shirt she'd changed into after work, deftly released the flap on her nursing bra and urged her fussing son to nurse himself back to sleep.

Liberty sighed. "Have I ever told you how jealous I am?"

Eden glanced up in surprise. "What? In the past thirty minutes you've decided you want kids?"

"No. I want bodacious boobs." She glanced at her own modest breasts and sighed again. "You think you'll get to keep yours when you stop breastfeeding?"

Too preoccupied by the conversation on the porch to smile, Eden answered distractedly. "I don't know. If they're a package deal with my new hips, I'll pass."

"Don't be silly. You look like Marilyn Monroe in *Gentlemen Prefer Blondes*. Men love that."

"Sure. Men born in 1932." Leaning her head against the cushioned back of the chair, she rocked gently. "Did you catch anything that was said on the porch, or were you in the back of the house?"

"Are you kidding?" Liberty plopped herself onto the bed. "The front door was open, so I sat on the couch and listened to everything."

"What about studying for your tests?"

"Oh, I learned plenty." She raised dark brows and swiveled in her chair.

Eden rolled her eyes. "Meaning? Or shouldn't I ask?"

"Meaning—" Liberty put her legs on the bed and crossed them beneath her "—that the two of you were doing a verbal dance that makes salsa look slow."

"*I* wasn't!" Eden protested.

"Oh, no? You want to tell me you weren't even a little hot and bothered over the boy?"

"Please." Eden rolled her head against the cushion. "I'm hot and bothered over everything lately."

"Still?"

Eden nodded. "Ironic, isn't it? I wouldn't do a thing about it now, not with Liam. Anyway, this is generic hot and botheredness. It's not about an individual. I'm going to see my doctor and tell her my hormones are still in an uproar."

"What? And ruin a perfectly good libido? Why not take advantage of it? You've been living like a nun for, what? Two years?"

"I like living this way. It keeps me sane. And I'm certainly not going to drag Liam through a series of boyfriend experiments. Romance is absolutely not my priority."

"Who said anything about romance?" Liberty grabbed a pillow, placed it on her lap and rested her elbows on it. "You forget that I sing the same song. I'm not in the market for marriage any more than you are. But we're young. Don't you want sex at least once more before you give it up in the interest of motherhood?"

Eden considered the question seriously. "Honestly? Looking back, I've always thought relationships were more bother than the sex was worth."

"That's not good." Liberty looked

thoughtful. "The big difference between you and me is that you've always had expectations, and I never have. Trust me, sex is much better when you don't care if Mr. Right Tonight is still with you in the morning."

"Hmm." Eden didn't completely discount what her friend had to say, but neither did she believe she had the right temperament for a one-night stand. In the past, her temporary liaisons had been flops. She shrugged. "It doesn't matter anyway, because with Liam—"

"Liam is a baby, who won't have any idea what you're doing right now. That makes this the perfect time to take advantage of your new—and possibly temporary—libido. Your son will never have to know. You deserve great sex before you turn celibate until his high-school graduation. It's empowering."

"It's complicated. First I'd have to find someone." She shook her head, swirling a finger through one of Liam's curls. "Nope, I'll be better off getting my hormones under control so I won't feel like turning into the parking lot every time I drive by a sex shop."

She raised her head to grin...and looked into the startled face of LJ Logan.

Chapter Four

His gaze drifted to Liam's downy head and her, uh, bodacious bosom.

When he cleared his throat, he sounded as awkward as she felt. "Excuse me. I, uh, wanted to let you know I put our glasses… the ones we drank from…in the…" He pointed in the correct direction, but couldn't find the word for the room. "Uh…"

"Kitchen?" Liberty supplied.

He had to think about it. "Yes. And then I was just going to say…"

"Goodbye?" she filled in again.

He nodded. "Right. Goodbye. Again."

Eden closed her eyes. "Just tell me one thing. Are you staring because you've caught me breastfeeding or because you heard what we were talking about?" Might as well know right up front how embarrassed she ought to be.

"I would say...both."

Embarrassment engulfed the trio—or at least two out of three—and silence reigned until Liberty tossed her pillow aside, stretched her legs then slapped both hands on her thighs.

"Well! Seems like a terrible time for me to leave, doesn't it?" She stood and looked cheerfully between Eden and LJ. "I'm heading to First Cup for a double shot. Maybe you two will still be here when I get back." She considered them a moment. "Possibly even in the same positions. Can I bring you anything? Latte? Chai? Iron supplement? You're looking a little peaked. No? All righty." She walked to the door, turned sideways to edge past LJ and whispered loudly to him in parting, "This isn't *that* embarrassing, you know. You should laugh about it when I leave."

Eden heard the scrape of her keys as she

scooped them off the dining room table and then the creaky opening and closing of the screen door.

"I wonder why I didn't hear it when you came in?" Eden murmured.

"Because I tried very hard to be quiet," LJ responded. "I thought you'd gotten the baby back to sleep and didn't want to wake him."

His gaze began to drift lower again until he jerked it back up. Somehow his discomfort began to lessen hers.

"Is this the first time you've seen a woman breastfeed?" It seemed unlikely in this day and age, but he tugged on his loose tie as if he felt a bit choked.

"It's not the first time I've *seen* it. It's the first time I've *watched*."

Eden felt another blush coming on, then reminded herself she was a doula, for pity's sake. A woman's body and the way it operated before, during and after pregnancy was her area of expertise. Breastfeeding was more natural than nine-tenths of the things people did in public. She'd breastfed comfortably and inconspicuously in her doctor's office, in a restaurant booth and, once, in a cozy chair tucked into a corner of the public library.

And now she really needed to change breasts. She gave herself a quick pop quiz. Multiple choice.

When confronted by a gorgeous man watching you breastfeed, do you:

A) Cover yourself and tell him to scram?

B) Continue to breastfeed, but drape yourself with diapers, baby blanket and, if available, a pup tent?

C) Pause to call the La Leche League and ask someone there for emergency advice? Or,

D) Behave as the mature, self-actualized woman you are and proceed with confidence?

She chose D.

Fortunately, she had large hands for a woman, which facilitated holding and maneuvering Liam securely.

Offering Liam a little encouragement to detach from her right breast, she let him rest atop the Boppy while she refastened her bra and allowed the T-shirt to drop into place. Giving his belly a brief, loud nuzzle as she transferred him to her left side, she settled him, lifted her T-shirt, unfastened the bra and kept her head down while she helped him latch on.

She didn't have to look up to know LJ watched her every move. She felt his frank gaze.

"If you're thinking about putting this in a commercial, forget about it."

She spoke lightly, to relieve some of the tension. When no response came, she did glance up and found him staring at her rather solemnly. Their gazes locked and suddenly, shockingly, the silence didn't seem unnatural at all.

Somewhere in Oregon, some poor shmuck is missing this moment.

That was LJ's uncensored thought as he watched Eden nuzzle her baby, put him against her breast and gently, gently twirl a finger through his baby curls. It was a surprising thought from a man who didn't want kids, but he figured that anyone out there in the world who had one sure as hell ought to witness this.

I really should put this in the commercial. No one would think of Robbie Logan or lawsuits or scandals while they're watching Eden. He'd never seen anything so perfectly natural, so quintessentially pure and female in all his life.

"Ow!" Eden jumped and pulled her son away from her bosom. "No biting!" She continued to cradle him, but LJ saw her eyes water. "He's getting teeth," she explained, "so he likes to experiment."

LJ winced on her behalf. Then, without thinking at all—if he had, he never would have made the move—he stepped closer, reached for the baby and lifted him to eye level. "Looks like you're going to need a lesson or two in how to treat your mother, my friend."

It occurred to LJ belatedly that he could have instigated quite a scene, but Liam didn't cry. His chubby hands reached for LJ's nose, his chubby feet kicked merrily at LJ's chest, and his cheeks dimpled as he grinned.

The baby certainly had her eyes and nose, but not her hair. LJ looked around Liam's squirming body. "Do you have a freckle on your neck, too?"

He was sorry immediately that he'd gone there. It seemed awkward as hell to mention the phantom father, and he was actually relieved when Eden answered, "No, but my mother does. And he has her smile almost exactly."

"Is your mother in Portland?"

"New Mexico," she answered as she rearranged her clothing. She remained seated as she gazed up at him. "I never would have guessed you've handled babies before."

He frowned. "I haven't." Suddenly he felt awkward. Holding a baby was like walking a tightrope for the first time: once you looked down and realized what you were doing, you were done for.

Apparently realizing his predicament, Eden laughed and stood. Coming close, she took the baby from his arms.

She smelled like lilacs.

"You're pretty enough to be the actress in the commercial."

He hadn't planned to say anything like that. He'd certainly never come on to a woman with a baby in her arms, but he supposed there was a first time for everything. The silence that descended was charged with energy, sexual on his part. Eden snuggled Liam close to her face, swaying gently. Her blue eyes looked absolutely huge as she gazed at LJ. He'd made her feel awkward, but he wasn't sorry he'd spoken. Listing her good points wasn't difficult at all.

Thankfully, a small, clear voice inside his head, as wise as Walter Cronkite, intervened. *Wrong time, wrong place. And, most unfortunately, wrong woman.*

He's flirting with me.

The realization made life a little more complicated for Eden. In the meeting this afternoon she'd wanted to swat him upside the head. Now he and his pheromones and his steady gaze were driving her nutty.

And those hands. They looked so strong, so trustworthy and capable of holding Liam. She had a swift dangerous image of those hands holding her, too, and the feeling that picture engendered was another thing entirely.

She and LJ Logan might disagree about business ideals, but physical sparks were flying all over the dang place. LJ seemed like a man with experience in physical-only relationships, and she was a woman with a whole lotta lust. Perhaps Liberty was right about this, and she should take advantage of the opportunity to have sex again before Liam was old enough to know what she was doing. In the brief-tryst department, she and LJ could be the perfect match.

She claimed to be uninterested in one-night stands, but, come to think of it, all her past relationships could be termed brief trysts. Regardless of her intention when a relationship began, none lasted very long. The disappointments piled up. That made a self-limiting fling like the one she could have with LJ all the more appealing…and practical. He'd return to New York—as expected. She'd carry on without him—as expected. And they'd never have to see each other again. No awkward chance encounters…and no hoped-for chance encounters, either.

How clean. How realistic.

She'd worked out their entire relationship including the breakup by the time LJ said, "He's asleep," pointing to the infant snuggled beneath her chin.

"I'd better put him down again," she whispered.

LJ nodded, but didn't say goodbye. He stood, staring at her until she thought he must be as reluctant to leave as she was to have him go.

"Are you still thirsty?" she asked, her flirting skills rustier than an old rake. LJ didn't seem to mind.

"I am," he said with far more enthusiasm than her herbal iced tea merited.

She pointed a shoulder toward the kitchen. "Do you mind helping yourself while I settle Liam in his crib?"

"I don't mind at all." He continued to gaze down, taller than she and much broader. She wasn't a small woman, but next to LJ she felt almost dainty.

Eden felt a very feminine thrill run through her body. "I'll meet you in the living room."

Eden sidestepped to the door and a put a hand on the knob. Taking the hint, LJ returned to the front of the house while she shut her bedroom door very gently. Laying Liam in his crib and covering him with a light blanket, she rushed to her dresser, checking her reflection in the mirror to evaluate her clothing for come-hither potential.

"Let's judge this on a sliding scale," she told her reflection, but the situation was not good. She had on a pair of loose capris she'd worn when her tummy first started showing and a T-shirt she used to wear to bed. It had been bumped to daytime duty because it covered her new larger proportions well. Both garments could use a hot iron.

Briefly she considered changing clothes, but how obvious would that be? Might as well take her lipstick and write "Do you want me?" across her forehead.

"I hope you know what you're doing," she whispered, shaking her head.

Her grandmother Verla, God rest her soul, used to say that when a person knew what made her stumble, she could avoid the rocks on her path. Eden had always stumbled over men. Men and the desire to be somebody's meant-to-be.

In her early relationships with men, she'd had the unfortunate need to convince herself that romance would end in hearts and flowers and yards of tulle. Never again would she let her desire for love lobotomize her, which was what happened when an intent gaze and a you're-the-only-one-for-me grin made her mind go spongy. She began to think like the heroine in an old-fashioned fairy tale, waiting for the prince. Waiting. Waiting.

Once upon a time she could have used a rescuer, but she had been forced to save herself. Now she knew that was the healthy way, the best way.

If she had a fling with LJ Here-Today-Gone-Tomorrow Logan, then she could indulge her teeming hormones and her need to be held without endangering her heart. It would be like having one last dessert and making it the very richest, very best before going on a strict diet.

In lieu of changing clothes, she settled for taking down her ponytail, plowing a brush through her thick hair and scraping it straight back from her forehead more neatly. Then she put on a little clear gloss, checked on Liam again and headed to the living room.

LJ was there, standing by the window to take advantage of what was left of the evening light as he leafed through a copy of *Pregnancy* magazine that had been lying on her coffee table.

Her heart began to pump in a not-at-all sane way when he looked up from the magazine with a genuinely baffled expression on his gorgeous mug.

"What the heck are inverted nipples?" he asked.

The tension left Eden in a delicious rush. He looked so worried.

"Have I ever seen one?"

Her laughter felt like the downhill side of a roller coaster—all fun and release. "I don't think so. You'd have known it."

Lowering the magazine and returning the smile, he said, "Sounds painful. Maybe I don't know women as well as I thought I did."

Maybe I'd like to fill you in. The thought popped up before she could censor herself.

Her dear, departed grandmother had told her, "A body can't control every blasted thing that comes to her mind, but she can sure as shootin' figure out when to keep her yap shut."

Instead of speaking, Eden walked to the floor lamp on the opposite side of the couch from where LJ stood. Turning on the light, she banished the more-intimate grays and lavenders of twilight.

LJ closed the magazine and tossed it onto the coffee table. "My mother raised me to have very good manners. A reasonably polite man would act as if he'd already forgotten what you said in your bedroom."

"How polite are you?"

Beneath dark brows, his eyelids lowered. "Mom would be so disappointed." Stepping around the table, he approached. "So you're attracted to me, but you don't date much."

She raised a hand and backed up a step. "I used to date a lot. Which is why I don't date anymore."

"Interesting."

"Also I'm in a vulnerable state hormonally. I could be attracted to anyone."

LJ came closer. "Do you know a fine sheen of perspiration breaks out every time we're within three feet of each other?"

"Well, thank you very much. If there's one thing a woman wants to hear a man tell her, it's that she's sweating!"

"I meant me."

The little smile he was so good at—the one that barely moved his mouth and made him look as if he was thinking all sorts of things he wouldn't say out loud—tantalized her.

"I'm going to be in town just until this project is finished." He'd practically read her mind.

"I was just thinking that myself." Her forehead creased as her mind whirred.

Lord, she hated being indecisive, but right

now her mind was flip-flopping between *I want him/I want him not* like a fish on a wet floor.

"I understand." LJ broke into her thoughts, his smile still in place. "Since we know an affair is out, it seems safe to tell you that hearing what you said in there—" he nodded in the direction of her bedroom "—is one of the more flattering things that's happened to me in a long time."

Hold the phone. Eden blinked, trying to work out the part where he'd said, *An affair is out.* When had they decided that?

Then she realized he'd taken her prior comment to mean that she didn't want a relationship with a man who would be leaving soon.

"For the record, you do some pretty outrageous things to my hormones, Ms. Carter. I've never been turned on before by a woman who was slaughtering my PR campaign."

She turned him on.

Hair the color of fine mahogany, eyes like autumn sky and a smile that poked gentle fun at the situation and at himself—he was the yummiest, best candy ever, and oh, she loved sugar.

He was here, he was available; he was leaving soon. Three plusses.

"I'm glad one of us is thinking clearly," he said. "Neither of us needs any complications right now. But another time, another place... I might not give up so easily."

His voice was a silky, promise-filled rumble, but Eden heard his point loud and clear: he was flirting, nothing more. He didn't need the "complication."

Regret swept her up, surprising her with its intensity. She'd heard that excuse before. Here was one more guy, a really interesting one, for whom she'd be an unwanted "complication."

She could tell him she wasn't interested in anything long-term; she could say she was glad he'd be leaving soon. But old pain made her tongue thick, her mind sluggish.

When she failed to respond, he gave a little sigh. "Back to the west side for me. Know anyplace I can get a decent burger?"

She shook her head, found a bit of voice. "I'm a vegetarian."

"Ah." He looked a little surprised. "And I love steak. It was never meant to be." With a final devastating smile, he walked to her front door, then glanced back. "Classic rock or country-western?"

"Celtic harp."

"Really? Big-city penthouse or mountain retreat?"

"Suburbs."

He winced. "Good night, Ms. Carter."

Eden practiced her best nonchalant shrug. "Good night, Mr. Logan."

Chapter Five

By noon the following day, LJ didn't feel remotely well. Something was burning a hole in his gut, and he figured it was either the barbecue bacon cheeseburger he'd had the night before or the conversation he was currently having with his uncle, Terrence Logan.

"I liked the commercials when you first showed them, LJ. I think we all did, and I don't want you to assume we don't appreciate the work you've done." Terrence sighed, glancing out the window of Papa Haydn's restaurant, where he'd invited his nephew to lunch and drinks. So far, they'd only taken advantage of the drinks.

LJ followed Terrence's gaze to the bustle on Portland's eclectically fashionable Northwest Twenty-third. The cold beer he'd ordered was not helping his stomach. Turning his head, he looked for the waitress so he could order an alternative drink. Maybe the restaurant served Maalox.

He'd had PR campaigns questioned before; it was part of the business. He'd worked like a dog, however, to impress his uncle. He'd traveled across the country when he was, in fact, swamped with business on the opposite coast. He didn't need this job.

What he needed was the opportunity to win his uncle's favor.

His father, Lawrence, Sr., and his uncle Terrence had been estranged since Lawrence wrote a nonfiction bestseller titled *The Most Important Thing.* In the book, Lawrence, a psychologist, presented strongly opinionated and well-crafted arguments for putting family ahead of work rather than the other way around.

After years of competition between the brothers, Terrence, a true workaholic, had viewed his brother's magnum opus as a direct attack.

Then tragedy had struck. Robbie Logan, Terrence's son, was kidnapped at six years old. According to Robbie's siblings, Terrence had feared the kidnapping was somehow divine punishment for not putting his family first. LJ's father had attempted to reconcile, to offer his support, but Terrence hadn't wanted to hear his brother's name spoken at that time. The pain ran too deep.

As an adult, Robbie had reunited with his family. LJ could see, however, that Terrence carried a pain, a deep grief similar to the one he saw in his own father.

LJ had hero-worshiped his dad forever, but in some ways he was more like his uncle. Terrence had a head for business and the drive to see his plans fulfilled. LJ's grandfather had taught by example, impressing upon his sons that a man's job was to nail down an excellent income. Unwittingly he'd set up a battle between his children—the businessman and the philosopher.

Now, two decades beyond the publication of Lawrence's book, the brothers were still engaged in a cold war, still hurt and wary and suffering from the estrangement.

Lawrence's blood sugar and cholesterol levels were up. He had hypertension that wasn't responding well to medication. Because he took good care of himself, LJ's brother Jake, the family M.D. and general buttinsky in all things medical, had suggested recently that stress might be the greatest contributing factor to their father's health concerns.

LJ, his brothers and his cousins wanted to put an end to the rift between their fathers.

Saving the Children's Connection, which was undeniably one of Terrence's babies, would be LJ's contribution. He was convinced Terrence would be more willing to talk about Lawrence when he considered LJ a trusted resource and even a kinsman.

LJ was a type-A guy, like his uncle.

Sometimes LJ thought his father seemed to feel almost guilty that the son who was named after him had somehow missed the most important message Lawrence believed he would ever teach: that career achievements and monetary success were nothing compared to the quieter daily joys found in a household.

Now LJ had a chance, possibly his first and last, to be his father's hero. All he had to do was end a two-decade-long feud.

Unfortunately, a distracting blonde with lots of opinions stood in his way.

"How many board members expressed opinions similar to Ms. Carter's?" LJ asked, engaging the supremely confident business-man inside him.

"They didn't express the same opinion Eden had, LJ. They expressed *concern* that she might have a point."

LJ fluffed the problem away with a wave of his hand. "In that case, let me talk to them again—without Ms. Carter. I'll explain a few basic tenets of marketing and promotion that she wasn't aware of when she spoke up."

Terrence started to shake his head before LJ finished. "The seeds are already planted. And the board knows and trusts Eden. She's calmed the fears of a number of our clients on a one-to-one level. Her perspective has to be counted. She's a—"

"Client, too," LJ finished for his uncle. "I know."

What did Terrence want him to do? Confer with Eden? He shook his head. This wasn't a college project. And if it were, Eden would be a poor choice for a partner. Back in college, he'd have had the hots for her all day long if they worked together.

"I want to schedule another meeting with the board. In the meantime, I'll have my team in New York work up an alternative commercial taking into account your concerns."

"That's fine. Excellent." Terrence began to look relieved. "To make sure all the concerns are addressed, because I'm sure you'll agree we can't waste any time, your aunt Leslie and I have come up with an idea we believe will help you address all issues."

LJ smiled politely. *More help. Just what I need.* With respect for his uncle's position, he inquired with as much interest as he could muster, "Tell me about it."

For the first time this afternoon, the frown between Terrence's brows softened. "I'm happy to be able to offer you one of the executive suites we keep at a fine inn at Canon Beach. Fully stocked minibar in the room, and the restaurants are all within walking distance. The service is always excellent. We've never had a complaint."

LJ began to wonder whether anyone in his family had a lick of business sense, Terrence included. "Uncle Terrence, I've got a job to do here. I haven't got time for a vacation."

Terrence's white brows rose. "You're not getting one! This is about work. You'll head down tomorrow and check in. Leslie thinks you should take the weekend to enjoy the coast, but that's up to you. Whether you decide to relax or work on your own Saturday and Sunday, you will, I hope, be prepared to have your first meeting Monday morning."

If possible, LJ's stomach grew unhappier. "First meeting," he began his question, every fiber of his being telling him he didn't want the answer, "with whom?"

Eden told herself she'd had a close call, a very close call indeed.

She'd made three postpartum home visits today, to women she'd followed all the way through their pregnancies. Two of the new mothers were doing well, but one was struggling with postpartum depression. Eden had prescribed herbs and supplements, brainstormed some additional child care options and suggested a support group for single moms of infants. The problem, though, appeared to be that the mom, Kasey, was afraid she'd never date again.

Join the club, Eden had wanted to say, but restrained herself. Not very compassionate. Kasey's loneliness and her strong desire to have a mate echoed off the walls of Eden's own world, making her grateful in the extreme that she had chosen, after her flirtation with LJ, not to attempt a relationship right now. She simply didn't need the drama.

As she returned to her office at the Children's Connection, she thanked her guardian angels for nipping the attraction to LJ in the bud.

She was over...mostly over...his rejection. All that mattered now was LJ's ability to create a campaign that held water.

"SMJ—save my job," she muttered as she opened the door to her beloved office.

The glass-covered blotter on Eden's desk sported pictures of the babies she'd helped bring into the world since becoming a doula. She hoped that someday she'd need an entire wall to represent all the mothers she'd coached.

Years ago Eden had lost faith in allopathic

medicine and traditional psychotherapy—
any modality, really, that thought it had all the
answers instead of seeking and trying out new
information. New and better ways to help.

Standing by while someone suffered or
while they begged for help that didn't come
filled her with outrage like nothing else
could. In her own practice, she studied every
day. The wall of bookshelves behind her
desk bore testimony to the new material she
gathered and read all the time. Homeopathy,
herbs, hypnosis, acupressure—she took advantage of it all, and loved to watch her
efforts ease the struggles of a difficult pregnancy or labor.

She was good at what she did, and so was
the Children's Connection. She didn't want
to see the clinic go down under the onslaught
of honest errors and ensuing awful publicity.

She didn't want to lose a job that made it
possible to be a single parent with on-site
day care and medical benefits. After an ado-
lescence filled with fear, never knowing what
to expect when the sun rose on a new day,
she craved consistency.

Boredom? Bring it on.

Placing the bag she carried to her appointments on the floor near a large basket of toys for smaller visitors, Eden slipped into her desk chair and prepared to sift through the tidy pile of messages she'd picked up from reception.

"Gina Noonan phoned. Ginger tea not helping nausea. Any suggestions?" Eden grabbed a pad of paper and scribbled a note, reminding herself to pack an acupressure cuff next time she visited Gina.

There was a request from Terrence Logan to call him when she got in, but the "urgent" box was not checked, so she shuffled to the next message.

"Bonnie Eames needs an appointment. Baby Charlie colicky. Bonnie can't remember how to perform infant massage." Eden made a note to check her calendar and to recommend a well-illustrated book for Bonnie. Next message…

"See me in my office. ASAP. LJ Logan."

Beg pardon? Eden lifted the message and stared at it, as if that might change its effect on her. Obviously penned quickly in hard, bold lines, the clipped order made her feel like a kid being summoned to the principal's office.

She ripped a sheet of blank paper off the small pad she was using and wrote "Kiss my ass," adding after a moment's consideration, "ASAP." Once she'd underlined the words a few times hard enough to make dents in the paper, however, she knew that she'd been raised with more courtesy than that, so she took another sheet off the pad and wrote "Ask me nicely." With that note tucked into an envelope bearing LJ's name, she asked the receptionist to make sure he got it.

Back in her office, she didn't have to wait long for a response. LJ appeared in the open doorway, looking as gorgeous as he had the day before, but without the inherent humor she liked in his smile. This time his lips wore no curve at all.

"I apologize for the abruptness of my note. Now will you please meet me in my office to discuss this situation?"

Eden raised a brow. Terse, to the point. Not a hint of the flirtatious hunk whose attentions had flattered her yesterday.

Ignoring the stab of disappointment, she replied, "Apology accepted, what's wrong with my office, and what situation?"

Crossing his arms, he leaned his shoulder

on the door frame and very deliberately scanned the room. "I can't have a serious business discussion with butterflies hanging from the ceiling."

Glancing up at the beautiful, sheer decorations that hung from hooks and swayed slightly from the air-conditioning, Eden said, "They're dragonflies. Babies love them. They're supposed to inspire serenity. Why don't you have a seat and see if they work?"

She held a hand out cordially, indicating the seat across from her, but he scowled.

"You're not upset about this?" Uncrossing his arms, he stepped into the room and closed the door behind him. "I can only conclude that you still believe you can create a better PR campaign than the team of professionals I hired out of business school. That, or you want a free vacation."

Eden watched him slip smoothly into the chair opposite her.

"English is my first language," she replied, "but I'll be darned if I understand a word you just said." Reaching into her top desk drawer, she took out a bag, tore it open and offered to share. "Hungry? I missed lunch."

LJ took the bag and looked inside,

frowning. "What is this? It looks like space food."

"Freeze-dried fruit bites. Yummy. And only two points for the entire bag."

LJ handed it back to her. "Now I'm the one who doesn't understand. Where did you get the idea you need to lose weight? I think you should eat real food, but that's way off topic."

Leaning back, he crossed his arms again and narrowed his eyes. "I'm not going to waste a week of work trying to explain marketing concepts. So this cockamamie idea of you and me working together on a PR campaign is out of the question."

Never a whiz at puzzles, Eden had trouble with this one until she remembered that Terrence had requested to speak with her. Munching her fruit bites, she pondered the situation.

LJ was ticked off about the idea of working with her, which was news to her, and Terrence wanted a meeting. Ergo, Terrence must have valued what she had to say yesterday and suggested that LJ listen to her concerns.

She gave LJ the squinty eye. "Well, my heavens, I don't blame you for not wanting to 'waste' a week explaining your business to me," she said, keeping her voice as sincere and neutral as possible. "Likewise I'm way too busy to waste time explaining our business to you. And, I figure it's up to you to do your own homework. Now what's this about a paid vacation? I have a note here to call Terrence, but you showed up first."

"I showed up first?" LJ looked chastised and ready to spit bullets at the same time. "You want another apology, don't you?"

Eden shrugged.

"All right. I'm sorry I jumped the gun and thought you and Terrence had worked this out between you before consulting me, but I am not going to work with you on a PR campaign, Eden."

She tilted her head. "Did you miss the part where I said I don't want to work with you, either, Junior?"

The wry smile from yesterday returned to his face. "No, I didn't miss that. Or the shot about doing my homework—which I assure you, I have done. And no one has called me 'Junior' since 1975. *Babe.*"

Eden winced. "Ouch. Okay, I apologize, too. Now, explain the part about the paid vacation."

He frowned. "Terrence has some wild idea

about sending us to Canon Beach to work in a more relaxed setting."

"He wants us to use the company suites? Together?"

"Separate suites."

Still way too close for comfort. "How long did he want us to stay at the coast?"

"A week."

"Oh, my God."

LJ nodded. "Yeah."

"Did you set him straight?"

"Yeah. No. I mean, I thought he'd already spoken to you and that you liked the idea."

Eden tossed back her head to laugh this time. "No. Oh, Lordy. I'll call and tell him it's a no go. Terrence is a sweetheart, but he gets some funny ideas sometimes. Don't worry," she added when he continued to frown.

Abruptly, LJ stood up. He paced a few steps, hands on his hips then turned to look at her. "When are you going to call?"

Beginning to suspect that yesterday's flirtation had been entirely about making sure she backed off his commercials, Eden tossed aside her fruit bites and picked the phone up with a snap. "Right now."

She punched nine then Terrence's extension and waited for the ring, giving the evil eye to LJ when he turned to examine a diagram of a womb. It was obvious he couldn't get her out of his hair fast enough today. This experience was so typical of her relationships with men: she'd never been able to tell the rotten apples from the ones that were good for her.

When Terrence answered the phone, she told him she'd received his note, that LJ was in her office to discuss the situation right now and that they both agreed it was an uncomfortable idea.

She listened, said, "Oh, reeeeaaaally?" and ignored LJ when he turned to look at her. "We'll meet you in your office in ten minutes."

To LJ's scowling countenance, she said, "Terrence says you seemed gung-ho about the idea over lunch."

LJ's mouth opened without emitting sound until he managed, "I thought you'd already said yes to the plan."

"And you didn't want to be the bad guy?"

"I wanted to talk to you so we could present a united front. It wouldn't have done any good for me to tell him it was a bad idea if you were packing your bags."

"Mr. Logan—" Eden slid her chair back from the desk and stood "—I like paid vacations as much as the next working girl, but I am not so hard up for a trip to the coast that I would persist in trying to change your mind about your ads."

She breezed past him, chin in the air. "Just make sure you save this clinic without my help, because I like my job."

She had no idea what this job meant to *him,* LJ thought as he followed her down the hallway, wishing he'd had the guts to veto the coast retreat without involving Eden further.

But when they walked into Terrence's office, Eden leading the way, he saw immediately that it wasn't only Terrence they were going to have to fight: Aunt Leslie was present, too.

Eden took the seat Terrence indicated, and LJ knew she had both barrels raised, ready to shoot the coast idea down. He recognized the truth, however, the moment he saw Leslie seated behind the desk, alongside her husband: it was all over except the packing.

Chapter Six

"I don't get it. Why couldn't you refuse? It's not as if traveling with your boss's nephew is part of your job description."

Eden shook her head at Liberty and folded her oldest cotton pajamas into her suitcase. "I'm not traveling with him. We're meeting at the inn."

"That's not what I meant." Liberty pulled the pajamas out and grimaced. "You're not going to work in your pajamas, right? Why get uglified when you have separate rooms? You do have separate rooms?"

"Of course." She snatched the pajamas back. "I like these. They're comfortable."

"They're green with yellow happy faces. They'd be ugly in the seventies. They're unforgivable now."

Eden frowned at the bottoms. "You're right. If I still thought LJ was charming, then I'd need the reminder that this is strictly business. Now that I know he flirted with me just to sweeten me up so I wouldn't mess with his commercial, I wouldn't touch him with a ten-foot pole." She nodded. "I can take my baby dolls."

"I still don't understand why you couldn't say no."

"I did. I told them he was right and that I didn't understand the first thing about PR campaigns. I even apologized for publicly criticizing his ideas."

"Wow. That must have made the man happy."

"It should have. But then he had to open his big yap."

Liberty went to the closet to riffle through Eden's better skirts. "And he said?"

"He said, 'I appreciate Eden's candor. I can see she's *excellent* at what she does.'

Which was a bold-faced suck-up lie because he's never seen me with a client. 'But it's clear that our jobs are very different. I think we both respect that we approach our work at the Children's Connection from two very different—'" she raised an index finger, as he had "'—but equally respectable points of view.'"

"Well, at least he was polite."

Eden humphed. "Yeah, he's good at that. But he might as well have handed a soup bone to a hound dog and told him not to chew on it. After Junior's speech, Terrence said, 'Two different points of view are exactly what we need on this project.' He said the business and the personal should be blended into one perspective."

"That's interesting." Liberty held out a swirly pink skirt festooned with a row of colorful sequins near the hem. "Why don't you take this? If the inn can recommend a babysitter, you might be able to have a nice meal out. Canon Beach has some great restaurants."

Food was the farthest thing from Eden's mind, but she said grimly, "Oh, I'll have a babysitter."

"They've hired a babysitter for you?"

Liberty looked impressed, but Eden shook her head, her smile brittle. "No, once Terrence made the comment about blending two points of view into one, Leslie jumped up and told him that was a wonderful idea and that we could take this opportunity at the coast to trade places."

That retrieved Liberty's focus from the perfect dining-out outfit. "How can you trade places?"

"According to Leslie, I can work on ideas for a boffo commercial while Junior plays single daddy. Leslie thinks it will help him understand our clients' needs. He and I are supposed to convene at the end of the week to pool our discoveries and make a presentation to the board of directors on our return home."

Eden offered her roommate a big, falsely enthusiastic smile. "Isn't that a great idea? Of course, we'll have throttled each other senseless by then."

Liberty gaped at her. "Trade places? It's like a reality TV show."

"Without a prize at the end."

"Junior agreed to this?"

"He smiled, shook hands with Terrence,

kissed Leslie on the cheek and hasn't been heard from since."

"Implying consent?"

Eden reached for the diaper bag she'd already loaded with infant Tylenol, diaper cream, homeopathic preparations and a nice big bottle of ibuprofen for her. Opening that container, she popped two pink pills in her mouth and chased them with a gulp of the herbal tea she'd set on her dresser.

"Implying," she said after she swallowed, "that the coast is going to be mighty stormy this week."

She tossed an extra pack of baby wipes into a second, larger diaper bag while Liberty studied swimsuits.

Eden shook her head emphatically at the bikini in Liberty's hands. "It's way too cold in April to swim in the ocean."

"But the inn may have a hot tub. Unless you plan to go nude."

"I don't plan to go at all. I can't take Liam in a hot tub. And I can't fit into that bikini." She took the bathing suits and shoved them back into the drawer.

Liberty removed a one-piece and stowed it in the suitcase next to the baby dolls.

"What really bothered me," Eden said, "was that for the first time, I saw how scared Terrence and Leslie are."

"You think they're afraid the Children's Connection might truly have to close?"

"I know their first concern is Robbie. Ever since that horrible article about him, he's withdrawn. He resigned, and Nancy is really worried. She's usually so focused, but lately when I see her at work she seems distracted."

"Nancy's the wife?"

"Yes. You hear way more about my work than you want to, don't you?"

Liberty grinned. "No. It's like an episode of *Grey's Anatomy*. I love it."

"We could use a little less drama." Eden sighed. "I just feel so bad for Terrence and Leslie. I'm sure they don't blame Robbie, but I think they're afraid the center may never recover its good reputation if they don't do some serious damage control now. Leslie went on about how we'll be able to relax at the coast when we're not working, and about how she hopes Junior will take this opportunity to familiarize himself with babies since they're our clients, too."

"And that's when Junior hit the road?"

"Pretty much. He kept this benign smile on his face, like he was agreeing but not really listening anymore."

"Probably in shock."

"Probably. When we left the office, he called me Ms. Carter and said he'd see me Monday."

"So you get the weekend off?"

"Apparently. Leslie said she hoped we'd use the weekend to relax and then get to work on Monday. She said she didn't think there was anything more restorative for a new mother than to fall asleep to the sound of the waves and to walk along the beach in the morning. She told me the reservations would begin tonight."

"Three nights of bliss before you have to deal with Junior."

"Right. And I intend to take advantage of them. I'll need the bliss to get me through the rest of the week."

In lieu of the "restful" weekend at the coast his aunt and uncle had planned, LJ spent his time on the Internet and at the central library, pouring over books and articles with titles like *Stress and the Single*

Mom, When All You Ever Wanted Turns Out To Be More Than You Can Handle, and *Fatherless Conception: New Trends in Pregnancy.* That last one contained interviews with women who offered their reasons for using clinics like the Children's Connection to be "alternatively inseminated" rather than waiting for a man to do the job. It wasn't easy reading. Made LJ feel positively objectified.

Shutting the cover of the tome he was currently studying—*Modern Conception: Not Your Mother's Pregnancy*—LJ rubbed his eyes and reached for the now-cold burger he'd picked up for dinner. A bite told him he'd either have to nuke his sandwich or swap it for a bowl of cereal.

Resting his elbows on the smoked glass dining table that came with his furnished Lake Oswego condo, he stared at his plate for much longer than necessary and in the end decided he wasn't hungry.

A vague—and, he was pretty certain, unwarranted—guilt spoiled his appetite. Eden Carter had shot him a look of such blatant panic when Leslie had suggested they switch jobs at the coast that he hadn't known whether to be insulted or relieved.

He'd decided he was relieved. If she didn't want to play the game, then she wouldn't be offended when he refused, as well.

The thing was, he'd had the impression she expected him to get them out of the mess they were in. He found that more than slightly ironic, considering she was the reason they were in this mess in the first place.

It was interesting that his first impression of her had been almost comically off base.

When she'd struggled through the meeting room doors, attempting to juggle plates of homemade cookies and her giant water bottle, he'd thought she was cutely awkward. Vulnerable.

She'd dispelled that notion quickly, exhibiting a spine of steel beneath that lush honey-coated exterior. The studying he'd been doing this weekend confirmed that his second impression was more accurate than the first.

According to his reading, the women who opted to conceive and give birth on their own, using a sperm bank, had to face scrutiny and quite often disapproval from their families, houses of worship and, sometimes, friends. Society at large was still suspicious of the process, and serious errors like the ones committed a few years back by the Children's Connection—specifically wherein one woman was inseminated with the wrong donor sperm—did not help matters.

It took nerve and it took great passion for a single woman to proceed with an alternative conception plan in the face of so many variables. Eden had both nerve and passion in abundance.

As he studied further, even scanning Internet bulletin boards visited by women choosing alternative insemination, he began to relate on some level. The women talked about yearning for family, living with the fear they would never realize their dreams, and finally deciding to take their futures into their own hands.

That part, at least, LJ understood.

Pushing his chair back, he stood and walked away from the table. The dining room looked out on Lake Oswego, rippling steadily in an April wind. Except for the undulating water, however, very little ever seemed to be disturbed in this part of town. Pots of flowers, whose continual vibrancy defied the seasons, hung from stoplights and streetlamps.

Homes sprawled along the shore across from LJ's condo. He had heard that the schools were great here and that it was a good place to raise a family, but there wasn't a lot of visual evidence where he stood, which suited him fine.

He didn't plan to raise a family. The best schools were of no concern. He didn't care where the supermarket was as long as he could order takeout.

He'd grown up, though, in a neighborhood similar to this one; perhaps not as affluent, but certainly well-to-do, attractive and well maintained. On his parents' front lawn, however, had stood a testimonial to the fact that their primary focus had been their children. Salvaged from a school playground, an enormous wood play structure had wreaked havoc with their curb appeal.

Adult neighbors had called it an eyesore. Local kids had loved it. Because there had been no room in the backyard, LJ's beloved late mother, Lisanne, had insisted that the structure remain in the front yard, then enlisted her sons and most of the neighborhood kids to help her sand and stain it, wrap some of the posts in live vines and paint flowers and bees on the tunnel slide. Then she held a "Grand Opening" party with hot dogs and Popsicles. LJ remembered that summer as one of the best in his life.

Always, even through high school, the Logans' home had been the go-to house in the neighborhood. Scooters, then bicycles and finally the junker cars high-school boys could afford had been parked out front through the years. Lisanne had routinely set an extra couple of places at dinner. His father had been on hand to fix bicycle chains, practice fast pitches and look over carburetors with kids he barely knew.

The apple, he acknowledged, turning from the window, *had fallen pretty far from the tree.*

Lisanne had passed on ten years ago, and Lawrence had since remarried to a woman with two children of her own. Amazingly he had managed to knit the new threads into the existing family pattern, formally adopting Suzie and Janet, who were Logans through and through. He'd canceled a long-planned work vacation in Europe to stay home and bond with his new family. He'd turned down a new book contract, because it would have necessitated spending too much time isolated in his home office.

LJ loved his home office.

To Lawrence, Sr., there was no such thing as too many family responsibilities. There was never a time when a personal interest or need eclipsed his family values.

It was an impossible standard for LJ to live up to.

The thought of building and maintaining family as his father had written about—as his father had done *twice*—made LJ feel like a failure before he began.

Feeling like a failure was not something he tolerated well, so he accepted that it wasn't in him to be a family man. He wasn't selfless. He didn't want it badly enough to change his life for it, and frankly he didn't intend to spend years suffering guilt because he knew he should do more, be more, give more. That would be a miserable way to live.

Leaving the dining area without another thought for his meal, LJ proceeded to his bedroom, where he planned to change into running clothes and pound some pavement through the streets of Lake Oswego.

In the hallway he passed a small table with a cordless phone and paused briefly, thinking it might be nice to talk to someone, but his brothers were absurdly busy with their own lives, and the women he dated understood that he wasn't the type to check in while he was away. Because it would set up expectations he had no intention of living by when he returned home, planned or spontaneous phone calls to women he dated were too dangerous a precedent to set.

He did have a conscience, after all.

Sighing like a dog with nothing to do, he reviewed his options—go for his jog, phone a family member, catch a movie alone or work so he'd be as prepared as possible come Monday. LJ chose work.

If his father knew, he would not approve.

But Lawrence, Sr., was in for a surprise, as this time all of LJ's work efforts were geared toward repairing the one relationship Larry had not been able to fix.

With renewed purpose, LJ returned to the dining table, shoved the cold burger farther aside and pulled his books closer. By Monday morning he'd know as much about single mothers, alternative conception and adoption as Eden Carter did.

The drive to Canon Beach took fewer than ninety minutes on Monday morning.

Energized by a brainstorm he'd had last night and by a subsequent excellent night's sleep, LJ's mood added luster to an otherwise dull April day.

He was certain now that he was on the right track with the Children's Connection campaign. In fact, his new ideas so outclassed the first ones that he felt almost glad Eden had shot them down. He wanted to make a couple of phone calls, do a little more research and then he'd call his team in New York, have them draw a few storyboards and FedEx them to the West Coast.

Suddenly, he was looking forward to the week in Canon Beach—great seafood, morning jogs on the sand, plenty of time to work, since Eden was no more interested in Aunt Leslie's harebrained "life swap" idea than he was.

It was noon by the time he'd settled himself in one of the apartment-style suites reserved for executives of the Children's Connection. He was ready to work, but his stomach had been growling for half an hour and on his way into town he'd passed a restaurant that advertised oyster po' boys.

Donning running shoes and a pair of navy sweats, more casual attire than he ever chose on a normal workday, he headed to town.

Because the Oregon rains were nowhere near ready yet to yield to summer, it was still off-season at the coast, and LJ's restaurant of choice had plenty of tables available. He chose one by the fireplace and settled in, ordering a beer and his oyster sandwich before he heard the baby cry.

Instinct told him not to glance over.

Temptation made him do it, anyway.

As soon as he got a good look at the woman waving a cracker with one hand while she dug through her purse with the other, instinct kicked in again and told him something was amiss with Eden Carter.

He'd never yet looked at her without feeling a burst of physical attraction.

Today it would have seemed almost, well, inconsiderate to desire the pretty but exhausted-looking single mother at the nearby table.

Her glorious hair had been pulled back with no thought of fashion. Her face, with its voluptuous features, showed fatigue and strain.

LJ's muscles began to vibrate with tension as he tried—he really did try—to mind his own business. He pictured the oyster sandwich, a cold beer, and after lunch an invigorating walk back to the inn....

Little Liam Carter whimpered some more. Loudly. LJ noticed a couple at another table shoot an irritated look in Eden's direction. Shooting an equally irritated look at the couple, LJ scraped back his chair and stood.

Damn it all! Eden's lower lip had started to quiver. Her pretty white teeth caught it. Even as LJ accepted his fate, he mourned the loss of his peaceful afternoon.

Keeping his gaze on her, he took a step toward her table. And had the frightening thought that if he got involved today with Eden Carter, he'd have a lot more than one afternoon to worry about.

* * *

"It's okay, sweetie, we'll leave in a sec. Mama just needs to pay our check and we can go back to the inn and take a nap."

As she said the words, Eden wanted to cry with exhaustion. Liam had been fussy and restless since they'd arrived Friday night. Since then, Eden had barely slept a wink, and she hadn't exactly stored up on shut-eye in the last several months.

"Have a biscuit, baby," she offered again, tempting him with Zwieback toast while she searched her purse. "Mmmm, so yummy. I know my wallet is in here somewhere…"

"Can I help?"

The perfect masculine timbre was unmistakable.

She froze, knowing of course that she would see LJ at some point this week, yet somehow unprepared for the encounter.

When she'd failed to run into him at all over the weekend, she'd begun to wonder if he intended to offer a passive protest by not showing up.

"Hello." She nodded, all her anxiety at having to endure this crazy week rising to the forefront the moment she actually laid eyes on him.

A simple pair of sweats looked excellent on the previously expensively suited LJ. With his thick, wind-mussed hair and sea-blue eyes, he looked as if he lived at the coast.

"You seem to have your hands full." He nodded at the Zwieback she'd been trying to use to pacify Liam, then pointed to the giant diaper bag she was trying to balance on her lap. "May I do something?"

In the eight months since Liam was born, only Liberty had been around to help with the daily dilemma of having twelve things to do at once and only two hands. At first, Eden looked at LJ blankly. Then she mumbled, "I'm looking for my wallet."

He nodded. She expected him to take the Zwieback, though it was already a bit soggy from one trip to Liam's mouth. It took a long moment for her to react, therefore, when LJ reached for the check on the edge of the table, turned it over to determine the cost of the meal and reached into his own pocket.

"No," she said when she regained her senses.

"Absolutely not. I mean, thank you, but—" she waggled the teething biscuit at him "—no."

"Your meal doesn't amount to ten dollars. I can handle it."

Ten dollars was nothing to sneeze at on a single mom's budget. LJ seemed cavalier about money in a way she, literally, could not afford to be. "Well, I can't handle it. I mean, I can't handle you paying for it. I've been supporting myself since I was seventeen, and I don't intend to stop now."

The frown that had been etched into his brow since he'd arrived at her table rose a notch. "Seventeen. I was in high school, wondering how to handle baseball practice, speech and debate and my classes. How did you wind up on your own at seventeen?"

"I didn't say I was on my own. I said I started supporting myself then." In fact, she'd been taking care of her mother for several years by then. "Anyway, the point is I ordered the food, and I'm perfectly capable." Leaving no room for further questioning, she thrust out her hand. "You could help me, though, by holding the biscuit."

He looked at the soggy baby toast in

distaste. "Why don't I cover the meal and you can pay me back?"

"I'm using my credit card this week. Do you take VISA?"

He sighed. "Nothing between us is going to be simple, is it?"

Chapter Seven

Eden knew this was not the time to back down. A single girl couldn't allow a man to pay for her meal without a good reason, because… Well, because. "It doesn't look like it," she said, answering his question.

Reaching for the diaper bag on her lap rather than the Zwieback in her hand, LJ set the bag on the table, opened it, dug around amongst the diapers, disposable bibs, changes of clothes and teething foods she routinely overpacked and finally withdrew a black-and-red wallet.

"This what you were looking for?"

"My hero," she murmured, in truth mightily relieved. Taking the wallet from him, she withdrew her credit card. "I think I'm supposed to pay at the cashier."

He waited for her as she donned her baby sling, lifted a still-unhappy Liam from the restaurant high chair and slipped him into the sling. Then she reached for the check, their jackets and the huge traveler diaper bag.

LJ made an expression of disgust. Without asking for permission this time, he grabbed the bag, slung it over his own shoulder and took the jackets out of her hand. When Eden began to protest—for good reason, she thought—he interrupted with, "You need help."

"Probably." Looking at the giant bag weighing down LJ's shoulder, she murmured, "I definitely need to pack less." Then she explained, "I parked our stroller at the front of the restaurant, so we're fine. And your lunch will be coming soon."

LJ hesitated only briefly. "I'll walk you to the door then."

He truly seemed intent on helping—a little grumpy about it, though, Eden thought. So, together they made their way to the cashier, where LJ waited while Eden paid her bill and added a tip to the credit card receipt.

"That's that," she told the man who held her belongings.

He made no move to give them back. "Where's the stroller?"

Eden pointed to the buggy folded and stored behind the hostess desk. She expected LJ to hand over her stuff and head back to his meal. Instead, he retrieved the stroller, asked her how it unfolded and, when she said she could handle it easily since she was used to it, he replied, "Just talk me through it, Carter."

Once the diaper bag and the jackets were stowed in the basket below the seat, Eden took the handlebar and said, "Thank you very much. Really. I bet your lunch has arrived. You're going to love the food."

LJ stared at the baby happily engaged now in teething on the top rail of the sling. "Are you going to put him in the stroller?"

"No. He's happier next to me. I bring the stroller mainly to carry our junk. By the time we reach the inn, he'll be napping."

LJ nodded, but he still didn't move. Clearly he was thinking something over.

When the pondering was done, he raised a finger. "Hang on a minute."

He returned when she was midway through her second yawn, Liam's head was beginning to bob against her chest, and she'd started to think about making a quick and easy escape.

The moment she saw him, carrying his lunch in a white to-go container, she knew that easy escape was out.

"I've got to pay the check, then I'll be right with you," he said, stopping briefly in front of her on his way to the cashier.

"You're not eating? But…that's silly. There's no reason for you to miss your lunch."

"I'm not. I'll have it in my room. Or on the patio. I have a great view of the beach. Do you?"

"Yes. But—"

"I'll pay the bill and be right back." He left her sputtering a protest to no one.

Upon his return, he commandeered the stroller, placed his meal carefully in the basket and headed down the sidewalk toward the inn.

She knew—and he must have known, too—that everyone who saw them assumed they were a family.

Eden hadn't been out and about as a typical nuclear family—mother, father and kids—in nearly twenty years. When a redheaded woman in her sixties grinned at them and said, "What a handsome family," Eden felt blindsided by a strong sense of satisfaction. Her self-esteem actually puffed up.

Surprised and dismayed, she ducked her head and walked a bit faster.

In her work she routinely encouraged other women to honor and respect the decision to become single parents. Single motherhood, she reminded herself vehemently, had been her *choice,* not a booby prize.

"You're not talking."

Quickly, she glanced at LJ. He was gazing ahead, pushing the stroller at a relaxed pace, but clearly aware of her.

"Neither are you." She paused. "Or were you? Talking to me, I mean?"

He looked right at her then and smiled, unperturbed. "You are a strikingly honest woman, aren't you?" He seemed amused. "You said exactly what you were thinking at the meeting when I made my presentation, and now you've as good as admitted that you're trying to ignore me."

"I'm not *trying* to," she denied, which made LJ laugh out loud.

"It comes naturally, eh?"

Eden grimaced. Liam was asleep, his head resting against her as she walked. Too bad he wasn't awake so she could play with him, give herself something to do. She felt as awkward as a newborn colt.

She wasn't half as honest as LJ speculated. No way was she going to admit how tempting it was to run with the redheaded woman's mistake and pretend for the rest of the walk home that she was part of a couple—with him.

It's a hangover from playing Barbie dolls as a kid, she told herself. Just your typical, "I'll be the mommy, you be the daddy and here's our baby" stuff. It would go away as soon as they got down to business and talked about how neither of them wanted to work with the other. That was a conversation they would have to start really, really soon.

Eden Carter looked about as fresh as eight-day-old bread.

Strolling beside her, LJ's initial impression on seeing her in the restaurant was reinforced by her too-rapid breathing, the tired circles beneath her eyes and the five yawns she'd been unable to contain since they'd left the restaurant.

He cared.

That was the scary part. Though her life had nothing whatsoever to do with him, though he had his own crazy schedule and arrow-sharp agenda to attend to, he wanted to ask if she had enough child care, whether she was getting any sleep, if she'd had her hormones checked.

It's the damned books.

When LJ studied, he *really* studied. The books he'd pored over this weekend had increased his knowledge and given him sympathy for single parents. Or maybe pity. After reading about the challenges, he knew he would opt to become a single father like he'd opt to become a skydiver without a parachute.

The moment he'd seen Eden in the restaurant, he'd felt uncomfortable. She was supposed to have been vacationing at the beach over the weekend. His absence should have facilitated that, actually. But instead of appearing refreshed by the sea air and two full days of relaxation, she looked exhausted.

Beside him, she cleared her throat. "The inn is very nice. Did you check in this morning?"

LJ felt a vague stab of guilt. He *could* have called to let her know he would be a no-show until today.

"Yeah." He steered the stroller around a woman who had bent to tie her toddler's shoe. "I went to the library over the weekend. I've been doing a little reading about mothers and babies." An understatement, but he didn't want to admit that he now knew everything about inverted nipples.

"Oh." Visibly surprised, Eden glanced up at him. "Were you, uh, preparing for this week?"

For the job swap. Was now the time to tell her he'd been studying so they wouldn't have to swap? That, in fact, he was pretty sure he'd come up with a new campaign even she would like?

"Actually," she said, before he could respond, "don't answer that. I know you're no more eager to give in to Terrence and Leslie's idea than I am. I'm sure you spent most of the weekend trying to come up with a way out of this situation. I have.

And here's what I think. I think that if you interview me—you know, ask me lots of questions about motherhood, and my choice to use a fertility clinic, you'll probably have enough information to fake your way through."

"*Fake* my way through?"

Of course that was exactly what he'd intended, but when she said it, it didn't sound so good.

"It'll work, believe me. I've thought it through. I even drew up a questionnaire. If you like it you can use it as a template for other interviewees."

"Other interviewees?"

"I've been thinking that you might want to talk to a few other women and couples who have used the center. I can put you in touch with clients who are aware of the problems the Children's Connection has had. Possibly even Meredith Malone, though we'll need to okay that with Terrence first, I'm sure. Meredith is the woman who received the wrong donor sperm. She has a beautiful little girl, though, as a result, and she's married now to Justin Weber, the clinic's attorney. She'd probably have great input on what it takes to reestablish trust and confidence in a facility after an issue like that."

LJ made a noncommittal sound in the back of his throat.

She was clever. He'd already decided to talk to other clients. Intended to take care of that this week, as a matter of fact, via phone and e-mail from the inn.

Apparently she'd been working as hard as he to avoid the job swap.

He stole a look at the sleeping baby. Couldn't blame a mother for being reluctant to allow just anyone to care for her son. He'd never thought much about child care, but he remembered his own parents taking him and his brothers everywhere—every dinner out, every vacation.

Eden glanced over to find him staring… and frowning. She looked concerned, as if she were afraid her efforts might be rebuffed. That and the fatigue so apparent in her face and the slope of her shoulders encouraged him not to reject her offer immediately. He had everything under control, but he could be a decent guy, too.

"So you even made up a questionnaire, huh?" He attempted to sound approving

"Yes. It's not that I don't think you can make up one of your own—"

"Of course not."

"—but I have a good idea of the issues that concern a woman when she's considering fertility clinics."

"Good point." He wanted to ask again why *she* had chosen a fertility clinic, but he doubted he'd receive any more of an answer this time. Eden Carter said what was on her mind, yes, but she didn't divulge personal information if she didn't want to. "Is that why you didn't sleep this weekend? Because you were working on the questionnaire?"

"Who says I didn't sleep?"

"Your eyes are telling me. I hope you weren't staying up all night."

They came to a corner. Cupping Liam's head with her hand, Eden stepped down carefully so she wouldn't jar him. It seemed to LJ to be a typically loving gesture toward her son.

Keeping her gaze straight ahead this time, she sighed. "I hardly slept a wink, but it wasn't because of the work. Liam teethed for a week, and even though he's sleeping pretty well again now, I'm not. It's a—"

"Pattern mothers get into. I know."

That drew her attention. LJ nodded. He really did know about this. "You've probably been in this no-sleep cycle longer than the past few days or even weeks, right? Especially if you're not a cry-it-out parent, and I'm guessing you're not, you've been out of the habit of getting a straight eight hours of sleep for how long? At least since the last few months of your pregnancy."

When they reached the next curb, she stepped up, then stopped to stare at him while he popped a wheelie with the stroller.

"Who have you been talking to?"

"Nobody. Yet. But books, the Internet— it's all there. Everything you need to know about parenting."

"Not everything." She begged to differ.

He grinned, delighted with the surprise on her honey-skinned face. "Okay. No, not everything."

She was like a master painter, he realized. To her, parenting was an art, not a craft.

"But I am impressed," she told him. "I didn't think—"

When she stopped abruptly, he knew just what she was going to say and congratulated himself that he was starting to read her fairly well.

"You didn't think that I cared enough to learn about it." He completed the sentence, catching her gaze and holding it. "I told you I care about my work. It's one of my top priorities. And I always go the extra mile for my top priorities."

They'd stopped walking. "Do you have many?" she asked. "Top priorities?"

"Very few. So when I focus on something—" he smiled "—I really focus."

He kept staring, deliberately, until she started to blush, a habit not shared by any of his female business acquaintances in New York. None of the women he'd ever dated blushed, either. At least, not that he noticed.

He nodded toward a building across the street, on the ocean side of the main road through Canon Beach. "The inn. Home sweet home."

"I'll put Liam down for a nap."

"And take one yourself?"

"I'm not the greatest napper." She patted her son's back. "He seems to have some sort of sensor that tells him when I'm asleep. That's when he wakes up."

Eden spoke with perfect acceptance, but LJ got angry. Actually angry. Not at Liam, certainly, but at the situation. One of his colleagues had had sleep apnea at night and actually dozed off at a stop sign during the day. Sleep deprivation from any cause was no laughing matter.

Where was Eden's support system? Where were the grandparents, the eager-to-hold-the-baby aunts and uncles who could give her a break?

He'd found one discussion board on the Net that devoted itself to exactly this topic: the need for new-mother backup.

"I bet you ordered something hot for lunch—probably French fries, right?—and now they're going to be cold and soggy. See what you get for being a Good Samaritan?" Eden shook her head and offered a smile. "Seriously, thanks for helping with the stroller, but I can take it from here."

She reached for the handles. When LJ made no move to let go, she prodded, "If you want to grab your lunch, we'll head to our room now."

He still didn't move. Not that he was trying to be contrary, but he was busy thinking.

"Tell you what," she said, "after I get Liam settled, I'll drop the questionnaire off at your suite and you can see if it works for you as a template."

"We're supposed to trade jobs this week. Not learn by interview."

He watched her brows rise and lower, her mouth open and close with no sound emerging before he added, "Terrence and Leslie were very clear in their request. Don't you think?"

"Their *request* was clear, yes. But you don't want...I mean...I..." She pressed her lips together, then obviously decided to talk turkey. "You sprinted out of that meeting. You don't want to trade jobs with me any more than I want to trade with you. You didn't even show up this weekend."

He raised a finger. "I was home, preparing. I was getting ready for the week."

The bold-faced lie didn't bother him. He didn't feel a twinge of guilt, in fact, because what he was about to do was 100 percent not in his own best interest.

"I came down here in good faith, believing you were prepared to follow through on Terrence and Leslie's plan, Eden. I'm ready to do what has to be done to make this campaign a success, and I thought you were, too, or frankly I'd have stayed in Portland."

"But you——"

"Who knows how many women and men will be affected by our decision? Taking care of Liam, familiarizing myself with the more…hands-on aspects of parenting could give me exactly the insight I need to kick this campaign in the a——" He glanced at Liam. "Into high gear. You said it yourself—when it comes to parenting, books will only carry a person so far. I need hands-on experience."

"What? Last Friday in my office you said——"

"If you feel uncomfortable letting me care for your son—even with you in the same hotel, close by and able to lend a hand if necessary—I appreciate that. Do you know that seven out of ten mothers feel guilty about leaving their kids with a sitter? Even when that sitter is a family member. And I'm virtually a stranger. One whose judgment you don't trust——"

"That wasn't what I——"

"So why should you trust me with your kid? Although I was a certified lifeguard, trained in CPR, and I'm willing to carry my pager and adhere to a set itinerary."

"Pager? I don't want you to take him—"

"Of course not. I understand completely."

"Wait a minute!" She closed one eye, like a pirate looking through a spyglass. "Are you trying to get *me* to say I'm not willing to trade jobs, so that *you* won't have to take any of the rap?" Both eyes went wide. She hissed to avoid waking the baby. "Mister, that is the most low-bellied, disappointing thing I have ever heard!"

"It would be, wouldn't it—*if* I were that underhanded. I might not even like myself. And I'm very fond of me." Shrugging, he smiled brightly. "Not a problem, because apparently my mind doesn't work nearly as deviously as yours does. I simply want to follow through with a job I agreed to."

Bending carefully so she wouldn't jostle Liam, Eden plucked LJ's lunch from the basket of the stroller. Less carefully she shoved it at him.

Reflexively he reached up to grab the white bag. When he released the stroller handles, she took them and began pushing the stroller across the street, toward the inn.

Obviously assuming he'd follow, she spoke without turning around.

"I must be having a mommy-brain moment, because I am recalling a conversation in my office during which you made it quite clear you did not want to be here with me this week. And now you're trying to make me believe you're ready to be Mr. Mom."

They reached the opposite curb, where she popped a wheelie as good as any of his and jumped the large stroller to the sidewalk without a problem. Heading straight for the front door, she kept talking.

"So who are you, really, Mr. Logan? Dr. Jekyll, the team player, or Mr. Hyde with something funny up his sleeve?"

With the stroller wheel nosing the door, she turned to look at him. Her firm lips said Tell me the truth. Her skeptical eyes said she wasn't going to believe him anyway.

LJ decided to go on lying a little longer.

"All I have up my sleeves are my arms. My only interest here is in executing the plans Terrence and Leslie put into place." He shrugged. "If you must know, I started to think maybe everyone was right, maybe I don't understand enough about your clients…enough about *you*."

He took a couple steps toward her, close enough to touch the top of Liam's back as he snuggled in his carrier.

"Maybe," he said softly, "helping out with this guy will better prepare me to address the clients' needs. And maybe it'll help me understand why you were so passionate about having one of these in the first place. That's got to help me come up with a persuasive campaign," he added softly. "Don't you think?"

Chapter Eight

She wasn't quite sure how it happened.

First she'd found herself agreeing to allow LJ to take care of Liam for a short time—she'd figured Junior would last an hour, max—under her strict supervision. They played in the inn's library, she and LJ kneeling on a soft rug in front of the fireplace while Liam practiced his crawling.

Then LJ had complained he wasn't getting a "realistic" enough feel for parenthood, so she'd agreed to wait in the lobby while he walked half a block away to get an ice cream while pushing Liam in the stroller.

Mission accomplished, he'd found her dozing in the lobby chairs and insisted she go upstairs to get some sleep while he watched the baby. When she refused, he told her to suit herself then casually asked whether she ever felt like a fraud teaching other mothers to take care of themselves while she wore herself to a frazzle even when people offered to help.

That had made her eyes tear up.

Heading to her room, big man and little baby in tow, she'd changed Liam's diaper with LJ observing closely, though not participating except to comment, "The kid must eat like a moose." After a guided tour of the diaper bag, this time with LJ insisting, "I know what a jar of baby food looks like," Eden released the most precious thing in her life to a man who held Liam at eye level and said, "Come on, killer, let's wander through town and break some hearts."

It was now two hours later. It had taken her a full hour of mental gymnastics to fall asleep, and she'd set the alarm for an hour after that. Sitting on the edge of the bed, her bare toes curled into the carpet and her shoulders hunched like an old woman, she was so groggy she could barely see straight.

She'd have been better off powering through her day as she usually did. Now she had to somehow shake off the lethargy and call LJ's cell phone to see where he and Liam were.

Before she could encourage her leaden arm to reach toward the phone, a key card slipped into the lock outside her door. She'd given LJ the spare, telling him to come back anytime he had to, whether she was sleeping or not.

Adrenaline did the job her mind alone could not.

Immediately she rose to her feet, hurrying to the door and flinging it open. LJ stood there, a baby dozing in perfect contentment against his shoulder, held by one big, secure arm.

LJ looked at her in surprise. "What are you doing up?"

"You're back."

She couldn't help the relief in her voice. When Liam was at the day care center, she knew where he was and that the people caring for him were diaper-changing, baby-feeding, tear-soothing experts. The only other person who had ever babysat Liam was

Liberty and then for no longer than the time
it took Eden to take a shower or have a dental
exam.

Attempting to make amends for sounding
amazed that they'd made it back alive, Eden
endeavored to sound clinical when she
asked, "How long has he been asleep?"

"Longer than you by the looks of it." LJ
didn't sound slighted at all, but he did seem
exasperated. "Have you slept at all?"

"Have I slept? Yes! Too long. I'm all—"
she waved a hand around her head "—discombobulated. This is why I do not nap."

"This is why you need to." Without
awaiting an invitation, LJ entered the room,
baby in his arms and diaper bag across his
shoulder. Setting the bag on the floor near the
bed, he carefully, very carefully, laid Liam
down in the center of the bed.

Exactly right, she mused.

Then he straightened, frowned and
reached for two of the four pillows on the
king-size bed. Stuffing a pillow on either
side of the baby, he nodded in satisfaction.
"That ought to hold him."

"Yeah, I'd say so." Understanding that
laughter would be inappropriate here, Eden

commented instead, "You seem very comfortable with Liam. I mean, even in the time you've been gone. You were holding him—" *Just like a daddy.* "Very comfortably."

LJ nodded. "Piece of cake. I only dropped him a couple of times, and if you comb his hair down from his forehead, you won't even notice the bump."

Instantly her gaze flew toward her sleeping son.

"I'm kidding." LJ relieved her concern before she started to babble about concussions and waking Liam up and where was the nearest emergency room?

"Everything went fine," he assured her. "I only came back because the battery was dead when I checked my cell phone. I was afraid you might have called and panicked, but in case you were still sleeping, I let myself in. Now," he said, "I would like to take Liam and let you sleep some more, but I'm pretty sure only one of us will agree to that idea."

"You've had him long enough." Eden walked toward LJ, shaking her head. "And I'm really grateful. And impressed. It really is…kind of cool of you to do this experiment for your aunt and uncle."

"Kind of cool?"

"Very cool."

"Very cool." He nodded. "I like being 'very' cool. I even like that you're impressed." His blue eyes glinted with male pride and unabashed enjoyment. "Don't be grateful, though. I told you that I'm doing this for me."

She'd stopped a few feet from him. He closed the gap by another foot. "When can I take him again?"

Was he joking? "LJ—"

"The little guy likes me. Really. I point out pretty girls." Stepping closer again, he lowered his voice. "I hope you won't get upset with him for this, but he told me things get a little dull in day care. And, he could use the male bonding time. Don't take it personally. You're still his first love."

Chapter Nine

Will the real LJ Logan please stand up?

Eden looked at her colleague's gorgeous charm-filled face.

In the old days, I'd have slept with him after the first date, she thought then amended that. In the old days she'd have slept with him before the first date was even over.

She'd looked for men who could make her forget her loneliness, her fear. Men who could relieve the burden of caring for a mother who'd been mentally ill to the point of becoming incapacitated for years.

LJ could so easily have been one of the

men she'd looked to for her own happy ending. The broad shoulders, the effortless masculinity and then the surprising kindness and humor—it drew her, washed over her like a wave and pulled her out to sea.

"I have to do some work on the PR campaign now," she said, an attempt to ground herself firmly in the present. To remind herself what this was truly all about. "If we're trading jobs, then I can't let Terrence and Leslie think you're the only one willing to bite the bullet."

The beautiful male lips curved gently. "You've got all week for that. I heard about a great Italian restaurant while I was out with Liam. How about if I stop by in a couple of hours and we walk there? It's close."

"You want to eat dinner together?"

"More fun than eating it alone. Uh-oh." He tipped his head slightly to the side, regarded her carefully. "You're about to say something like, 'I'd love to, but I'm still full from lunch,' and then I'll have to admit that I didn't eat my lunch, because you were right—oyster po' boys are terrible cold. And then you'll remember that I had to argue with you—a little—about whether we were going to fulfill Terrence and Leslie's request, which ate up a bit of time and made it impossible to eat my cold sandwich and soggy fries."

Crossing his arms, he rocked back on his heels and shook his head. "You'll start to feel guilty—don't deny it, everything shows up on your face—and even though I'll say, 'No. Hey, it wasn't your fault,' you'll agree to dinner out of guilt alone. And that, my friend and partner for a week, is no way to eat a Stromboli. That's what we're having tonight, by the way. Strombolis."

She shook her head. "That was masterful. Really an A-plus effort." He tried to look as if he didn't know what she was talking about, but he couldn't disguise a small, victorious smile. She sighed. "But I really don't want a Stromboli."

A flash of male stubbornness in his expression told her that his request had been more than casual. She smiled. "I'm sorry, but nope, no Stromboli for this girl."

She heard the breathlessness in her own voice, felt the flutter of her heart. Darned if she wanted to come across as weak, so when she spoke again, she made certain she answered more forcefully. "I'll have eggplant parmigiana," she stated. "And just for the record, I'm not going because I'd feel guilty if I didn't, Mr. Logan. I'm going because I want to."

Two days later they'd hiked in Ecola State Park, shuffled through the sand to get to Haystack Rock and watched their footprints disappear as the icy surf surged smoothly across the beach.

Together they'd introduced Liam to the sound of his first seashell.

Instead of working during the day, LJ stayed up late at night. There was no point in trying to sleep, anyway. All he thought about the moment he saw his king-size bed was Eden.

In her presence he behaved like a normal human, a gentleman and business associate. But underneath, he was no saner than a teenager, driven by an attraction that felt like a crush. It had him fantasizing about more than sex, though that was number one on his hit parade of daydreams. And night dreams.

He'd replayed her comment a hundred times over in his head. *I'm not going to dinner with you because I'd feel guilty if I didn't. I'm going because I want to.*

Taking the weight of his head in his hands, he slouched at the dining table in his suite. Storyboards and notes lay before him, ready to be polished, improved upon or reframed, but it was midnight now and he hadn't managed a lick of work yet. She'd shot his concentration all to hell.

In truth, taking care of Liam that first afternoon had been a lesson in frustration. And confusion. And humility. Just as LJ decided his stroll through town with baby was going to be picture perfect, the little guy had started crying. Howling. Wailing like a banshee. Why did the sound seem so much louder when you were responsible for calming it?

As they'd only been gone fifteen minutes, LJ hadn't wanted to return to the inn, thereby ruining Eden's nap and admitting that twenty pounds of trouble had defeated him inside a quarter of an hour. Lost for a solution, but determined, he'd picked Liam up and jiggled him. The baby's face turned beet red as he geared up for the silent scream. Desperate, LJ resorted to baby talk. One tiny fist shot out and connected with his nose. LJ walked up and down the streets of Canon Beach pushing a stroller with one hand and carrying a furious baby with the other until finally he passed a bakery and ducked inside.

"Give me anything you think he'll eat," he hollered to the woman behind the counter in lieu of a greeting. She must have had kids— and a husband—because she smiled, grabbed a big sugar cookie and passed it across the counter with the assurance, "It's on the house."

Searching for more than the two ineffective-looking teeth on Liam's bottom gums, LJ hoped for the best and waved the cookie beneath Liam's nose. As Liam's interest peaked, the screams subsided. Soon the baby was gumming the edge of the cookie and sending a cascade of gooey drool down his own clothing and onto LJ's. Never had LJ cared less about his appearance.

"It's working!" he shouted, as triumphant as if they'd discovered penicillin. When Liam grabbed the cookie, LJ reached for his wallet and looked expectantly at the clerk. "How many of those cookies have you got?"

Now he carried one cookie with him at all times, and Liam offered a big, gummy grin the moment LJ came into view.

LJ was getting used to having a baby

around. He even kind of really sort of liked it sometimes.

He liked it when he caught Eden smiling as he talked nonsense to a nine-month-old.

He liked the way she referred to him and Liam together as "the boys." Call him soft in the head, but he even liked distracting Liam's top half while she gratefully changed the bottom half. He just liked being around them. Yep, his concentration for work was kaput.

Eden had acted utterly appropriately every time they'd been together. But there were currents running between them.

Currents. He'd never let "currents" get in the way of his career before. He wasn't going to this time.

Wagging his head, he sat up, stretched his arms and determinedly picked up a pencil to get to work.

Just as quickly, he tossed it onto a storyboard depicting the frames of the new commercial he was working on. He still hadn't sent anything to New York to be drawn up more elegantly, because every night that he sat down to work he felt dissatisfied with what he'd done the night before.

Parenthood obviously wasn't the flower-studded frolic in the park he and his team had first depicted. Come to think of it, not one of them had a kid, so as of this moment he had the most hands-on experience. If anyone asked, he could tell them firsthand there was no way to simply define the experience of caring for twenty pounds of crying, wet-raspberry-blowing, giggling, snuggling, constantly peeing and endlessly in-need-of-something baby.

Spending time with Liam was confusing him as much as spending time with Liam's mama.

LJ had expected babysitting to be a kind of impersonal chore. Change the diaper, stroll the kid around, feed it if necessary, try not to be too bothered by the crying.

The first day with Liam, he'd hit the local bookstore and asked for the best baby book they had. In it he'd read that sometimes babies cried for no reason and not to let it get to him if he couldn't figure out a cause and solve the problem. The book must have been written for women.

As a guy, he'd absolutely seen the crying as a problem that needed to be fixed. He'd hung in there with the biggest baby's mouth this side of anywhere, but, damn, it had just about driven him loony until he'd finally made some really stupid faces and collected his reward: a gummy smile and joyful giggle that had felt like as much of a triumph as the day he'd opened his own business.

He would never admit that to anyone.

Sighing, he contemplated driving as far as he had to for a strong cup of coffee, but was sidetracked by a virtual wail from the room next door.

Liam.

LJ didn't pause to think. He jumped up, left his suite and was knocking on Eden's door in seconds.

It took a moment for her to answer. The crying intensified the closer she got to the door, and when it opened she had Liam bundled against her, his bright red, squalling face dripping drool on her shoulder.

She began to speak before she'd even gotten a good look at LJ.

"I'm very sorry. I know it's late. I'll try to—"

LJ swore. "Don't apologize. And don't open the door this time of night without even asking who's there."

Her eyes widened. "LJ." Relief washed over her. Peering around him to see if one of the other two doors on this floor was about to open, she grabbed his wrist and pulled him inside.

Bath scents from earlier in the evening lingered in her room. Eden stood barefoot, dressed in a thin, bosom-cupping shift that reached only to midthigh. Silky, firm, shapely midthigh.

Great gams.

Okay, so now he knew what they looked like above the shin. He could put that out of his mind, though.

"Heaven above, I'm so glad it was you."

Patting Liam and swaying side to side, she gave LJ a wan smile. The low-pitched, subtle accent that reminded him of biscuits and honey was more pronounced tonight.

"The woman across the hall has migraines. I gave her some peppermint oil to rub on her temples, but Liam's crying isn't going to help any. Shhh, baby, you're safe," she said, stroking the little guy's florid cheeks. "You're with Mama. You're fine."

Her crooning drew his attention to the baby, whose chubby fist clutched Eden's nightgown. LJ got a great peek at a breast that looked as if Botticelli had painted it.

He wasn't going to be able to forget that. He was only human.

"Eden." He cleared his throat and tried again when his voice got stuck in the vicinity of his Adam's apple. "Eden, no matter who you thought was at your door—the woman with the migraine—"

"I thought it was her husband."

"That's worse! Do not open your door without asking who's there. No—" he corrected himself "—do not open your door *at all* at midnight! Do you do that at home?" Did people come to her door at midnight when she was home? "You need a dog."

"I don't have time for a dog. It wouldn't be fair. But you're right, and I'm usually much more careful." She smiled again, then jiggled Liam up and down when his crying intensified.

LJ's gaze was glued to her breasts. Dear God, if he were as close to her chest as Liam, he certainly wouldn't be complaining. Clearing his tight throat, he asked, "What's the matter with him? Nightmare?"

"I think so. I don't know. He was sleeping

so soundly. He's not wet or hungry. I tried breastfeeding."

He did not want to picture that, so out of self-defense he reached for the baby. "May I?"

Surprised, she nonetheless released her son to LJ.

Now what're you gonna do? a voice taunted, but since trying to calm Liam took the focus off of trying to calm himself, LJ held the baby up and looked him in the eye.

"It's late," he said. "Man to man, this is no way to win friends and influence people."

Liam shook his fists and cried harder.

"Maybe I'd better—" Eden began, but LJ figured he and the little guy already had an understanding.

Using the hold that had worked on Liam a couple of times before, he palmed the back of the baby's head and used his other hand to support Liam's bottom and back. He continued to look into the liquid-blue eyes.

"Remember what we talked about? If you let your mom sleep tonight, I will personally introduce you to your first Oreo Blizzard when we get back to Portland."

"You will not!"

"Shh. It's working."

It kinda *was* working.

Eden controlled herself and let LJ do his thing. He kept looking Liam in the eye and kept speaking in that low, calm, masculine voice that was, Eden thought, even more effective with women than with infants, and soon Liam's crying subsided to disgruntled hiccups.

For days now, she'd been resisting LJ's spell, though she was glad her son had no such agenda.

As LJ quieted her boy, Eden's toes curled into the soft carpet, and tingles raced along her skin.

Liam won't remember this. But I'll never be able to forget.

This week she'd watched a man treat her son as if he were his own. The feelings LJ's actions engendered would completely mess with her mind if she let them, so she wasn't about to analyze anything. She didn't want to ask herself any questions when this week was over.

Once they were home, she did not want to sit in her rocking chair late at night and wonder again if she'd made the right choices—not about bringing Liam into the world, but about her own resistance to giving him a father. Watching a man's strong hands hold her baby caused such a pang in her heart, such a fearful yearning that she wondered if she was being horribly unfair to her own flesh and blood.

Eden's mother had remained single after Eden's father had taken off, then married again, briefly when Eden was eight. They had enjoyed two—exactly two—golden years of family before her stepfather left. After that, her life and her mother's simply unraveled. Her mother's manic depression worsened, and within months of her stepfather's departure, Eden became the mom and Gwen the child.

From ten to seventeen, Eden fended mostly for herself and for her mother, too. The memory of "the good years," as she'd often thought of them, were first a solace and then a torment. It might have been easier not to know what she was missing.

It took many more years for Eden to be rock-solid certain she could be a good mother, one who would be there every day of her child's life. She'd come to trust that she was capable of creating a family on her own, with the help of her friends.

Watching LJ with Liam rocked her confidence. Watching LJ made her *want*.

Father and son…

Man, woman, child…

Man and woman.

With LJ involved, any and all of those combinations seemed like the golden ticket.

His voice rolled over her, an unpredicted comfort for her, as well as Liam. "That's right, calm as air. You just relax, buddy. That's what nighttime is for."

That's not all it's for.

"You ready to hit the sack again?" LJ walked Liam to the window and pushed aside the heavy privacy curtain. "See? Moon's out. Stars are out. Time for all perfect babies to be in bed." He murmured quietly for a few moments then turned toward Eden. "Why don't you douse all but the light on the desk? I think he's going to drift off in a minute."

Unbelievable. Eden mentally pinched herself as she dimmed the bedside light she'd flicked on when Liam had started crying.

If anyone had told me last week that LJ Logan would be calming my baby, she thought, *and in the middle of the night yet, I'd have laughed myself silly.*

LJ moved toward the bed. Eden met him halfway to take Liam and continue the job of lulling her son to sleep.

The transfer of the baby from his arms to hers was surprisingly smooth. *As if we've been doing it for months.* She felt a bit self-conscious, but not awkward at all as she settled herself and Liam on the bed so she could nurse him back to sleep. She didn't even bother to tell LJ to leave. They'd gone too far for that.

Eden thought she understood now how the participants of reality TV shows felt. Thrown together in awkward situations, they formed bonds that seemed closer than they might have been under normal circumstances. Partly friends, partly playmates and mostly business associates, though they hadn't focused much on that recently, she and LJ had found a level of comfort disturbed only by their physical awareness of each other.

Not that he seemed terribly disturbed. Either he was used to a certain level of physical arousal or the one she inspired wasn't very troubling.

She sighed, waiting for him to focus his attention on something, giving her privacy while she settled Liam at her breast. She'd breastfed in his presence a couple of times this week, but he'd never stared as he had the first time.

True to form, he wandered to the desk and gazed at the work she'd laid out there.

Eden's heart skittered unevenly. Inspired by the most consistent napping she'd done since Liam's birth, she'd started working on ideas for the Children's Connection campaign. Placing calls to the same people she'd suggested LJ contact, she had culled ideas to address the clinic's most pressing PR concerns. She'd found herself engrossed in the work, but it was harder than she'd suspected. Now she worried that her efforts might appear foolish to a professional PR man like LJ.

He moved the papers around, lifted a couple. Studied them.

Liam fell asleep again quickly, so Eden positioned him safely on the large mattress, rearranged her bodice and stood.

LJ turned when he heard her. "You've been working on your part of the trade."

"Fair is fair." She shrugged, resisting the urge to downplay her efforts. "I called a friend of mine who's been producing commercials since college, and she explained storyboards to me, but I have no idea if I did it properly."

"At this point the idea is more important than the execution."

That sounded like a supportive statement, but LJ mumbled it with his head down, gazing at a sheet with some of the dialogue she'd brainstormed.

"You're thinking of using the actual clients." He looked up at her.

"Well, I thought an interview-style ad could work."

"I've been thinking the same thing, but I thought we'd use actors. 'Real-looking' actors," he added, responding to her original objection about overly-glamorous types. "Using clients who have good reason to remain disgruntled with the clinic seems like a risky proposition."

"I know. But..." She hesitated, wondering if she'd carried the job trade a bit too far. "I actually phoned a couple of them already. I based the dialogue on our conversations.

They'll be honest but supportive. I think you'll be surprised."

He laughed, but to Eden the sound didn't seem very humor filled. "After this week, nothing is going to surprise me." Glancing at the pages in his hands then back at her, he said, "It seems as if our work is almost done here."

Taken aback by the abruptness of the comment, Eden automatically contradicted, "We have three days left."

LJ's classic charming smile reappeared, but it seemed strained, effortful.

"We don't need the extra time." He raised the papers. "It appears you may have solved our problem, Ms. Carter. With your permission, of course, I'll fax these to my team in New York and put them to work."

"You like my ideas?"

"They're something to work with. They're fine." This time he sounded noncommittal, but picked through several more sheets, keeping what he wanted, leaving the others on the desk. "So I'll take these with me and fax them?"

"Yes, of course."

"Better get some rest." He glanced to the

bed, where Liam was already breathing deeply, puffing his lips out with each breath. "I'm sure Terrence and Leslie will encourage you to stay the rest of the week. Now that we've accomplished our goals, though, I'll be heading back in the morning."

Chapter Ten

He had changed completely in the space of a few minutes. Eden didn't understand LJ's conversion from Mr. Wonderful to ultracool businessman.

She realized that he was wearing a pair of drawstring pants that might have been pajama bottoms, might have been light-weight sweats. A plain gray T-shirt covered his torso.

She was wearing her baby dolls.

Company manners seemed misplaced, so she crossed her arms and insisted stubbornly, "If you're leaving, I'm leaving. I'm not going to laze around here while you go back to work."

"The definition of a working mother is that you're always working, correct? I don't think anyone is going to accuse you of lazing around. Take the extra time. No one will begrudge you."

"Why aren't you taking the extra time, then?"

"I'm in Oregon to work, Eden. I live in New York. I take my vacations in the Hamptons or on Martha's Vineyard, and I usually take them alone. I find it easier to relax."

Talk about hitting a person over the head to make your point.

Every bit of attraction she'd felt for him, every single bit of it felt like an embarrassment now. He couldn't have pushed her farther away if he'd taken his hand and shoved.

As they spent time together this week, she had been careful not to flirt, not to let her interest show even though she was fairly certain he returned the feeling. Why did he feel the need to distance himself?

"You know, Dr. Jekyll," she said, not caring if her hurt showed, "I really liked you this week. You were fun to be with. You've gone out of your way to let me rest, and you're surprisingly great with Liam."

"All part of the job."

"But now you're about as friendly as a por-cupine with a foxtail up his nose!" His last comment just made her angrier. "I don't know what your problem is—"

Maybe he's afraid you've gotten the wrong idea; maybe he's trying to be kind.

Some—not all, but some—of the hurt went out of her.

Liberty's accusation that she lacked good interpersonal skills when it came to men nibbled at the edges of her mind. If she said nothing, simply let LJ walk out, she'd nurse a mighty powerful resentment the next time she saw him. Then she'd either smile and ignore him as much as possible or whip out a few snappy hurtful comments when she could. Either way, she'd diminish herself. She'd diminish what had happened here this week.

They'd become friends of a sort. And she'd had the opportunity to watch her son bond with a father figure.

I've got to get Liam one of those, she

thought. *A male friend who can be a daddy figure.* Darn shame they couldn't be ordered at Babies "R" Us.

In the meantime, she had something to say.

Looking Lawrence Logan, Jr., straight in the eye, she took a breath and took the plunge.

"You can tell me and tell yourself that this week was all about business for you, but no one is that good an actor. You like Liam. I see that you're afraid we'll get too clingy or dependent on you or whatever, and I know you've sensed that I'm a little bit attracted to you—just a little. You're nice, but you're no John Corbett. But you can rest assured that I have *no* designs on you as a husband or daddy for Liam. You don't need to get all cold and distancing. We can say goodbye nicely."

"Who's John Corbett?"

Not the response she expected, but oo-kay. "*My Big Fat Greek Wedding.* He was the groom. Now he's singing country. How sexy is that? And he dates Bo Derek, a woman his own age."

"And I'm not as attractive as he is?"

Eden had never seen John Corbett in

person and had no idea whether he was good with kids, but if she had to guess she'd say that side-by-side LJ would make poor John appear positively pale.

Aloud she said, "No. I'm sorry."

"Hmm." He appeared to give that some serious consideration. "If John were here, what would he do right now?"

"He'd…be personable."

LJ's eyes looked stormy, very April-at-the-coast, as he took a step toward her. At least, she thought he took a step; she didn't see it, but he seemed closer. "Personal?"

Suddenly he was very, very close indeed, and the room felt so hot she couldn't even concentrate on being offended.

He gave her a moment to reject his kiss if she wanted to, a fraction of a pause before he slipped one hand behind her back and pulled her into his body.

Eden felt as if she were at the top of a roller coaster, about to plunge into the breathless unknown. On that kind of ride, you didn't tell the roller coaster to turn back at the top of the peak, so when LJ clasped her and lowered his head, she encircled his neck with her arms and lifted her face.

The first touch of his lips sent her diving recklessly into the ride.

LJ, on the other hand, worked the controls.

He tasted her as if she were wine, studying and savoring, controlling the depth of the kiss. When the pressure of his lips increased and she felt the first nudge instructing her to open her mouth, Eden felt heat in her belly and flooding her legs. This was every bit as good as she'd fantasized it would be.

Then one of LJ's large hands moved confidently from her back to her breast, and she thought, *Better. This is way, way better than I fantasized.*

He seemed to know exactly how to touch her, covering her with his palm, kneading gently and then with more force as the kiss deepened.

When his tongue filled her mouth, she wasn't sure she could remain standing.

Still in control, LJ stopped exploring and began to take what he wanted, moving in her mouth and touching her breast exactly as he pleased. She could tell he was filling his senses with her, wanting her from a very fundamental place. It excited her beyond reason when his free hand slid down to grasp her bottom so he could press her still closer.

LJ must have known how far he could go before he had to stop, and obviously he realized he'd reached that point.

It was with a mix of frustration, regret and a relief born of practicality that Eden felt LJ's hands firmly circle her arms and set her slightly apart from him.

His head remained lowered, and when stars stopped circling her dizzy brain, she realized he was breathing as hard as she.

"How's that for personal?" he asked.

"Fine," she breathed. "But I said 'personable.'"

He grinned. "I know."

Their laughter blended, rich but low so they wouldn't disturb Liam. As they calmed, LJ asked, "Do you want to talk about what just happened?"

She shook her head. "Not particularly, no."

"Do you want to go out once we're back in Portland?"

She let her heart answer. "Yes."

"Good." He seemed almost surprised. Pleased. "Get a babysitter."

* * *

They were back in Portland four days before Eden saw LJ again.

He called a meeting of the board members and any Children's Connection staff that wished to attend. Essentially the same people who'd attended the first meeting assembled once again to listen to LJ's plans for restoring the Children's Connection's public image.

Eden had considered staying away this time. Her presence had certainly wreaked havoc previously.

Also, she hadn't seen LJ since The Kiss, and she didn't think she wanted to meet with him for the first time in a public forum. She'd had some time to think about the date he'd promised her and to consider all the implications.

A babysitter wasn't the only thing she'd have to get.

She hadn't been on birth control in ages. Her ob-gyn worked out of Portland General. Eden had run into her in the cafeteria more than once. Though she felt foolish and immature for thinking this way, she had the odd notion that the minute she asked for birth control, the entire population of Portland General Hospital, including the Children's Connection staff and LJ's relatives, would know she was planning to sleep with him.

She wanted to confirm their date before she addressed the birth control issue.

For that reason more than anything, she'd planned to be busy elsewhere during the meeting, but then LJ sent her a memo requesting that she "be on time, bring more cookies and take a seat at the front."

Appropriately, the memo made no mention of his feeling hotter than a four-alarm fire every time he thought of her. She certainly hoped, however, that he was feeling that way. Lordy knew she was.

It was exciting and scary to feel such attraction and such urgency, as if she had to ensure their affair before either of them changed their minds.

I don't want to change my mind, she thought. *I want to find out what happens when desire is this strong.*

Sitting in the boardroom at the head of the table as he'd requested, she realized she'd never felt such a physical attraction before, or one that was independent of her girlhood

desire to be plucked from the reality of life
and carried to a place where every day was
a love-filled paradise. As if that existed.

She'd had therapy two days a week for a
year before she'd conceived Liam. She'd
wanted to make certain, a hundred-and-ten-
percent certain, that she was ready to live
free from the fears of her past. And free from
the fantasies.

LJ Logan was not her knight in shining
armor.

He was a treat, like splurging on a fabulous
dress as a reward for working hard.

According to Dianna March, who was
seated halfway down the table on Eden's
right, LJ had returned to the office he was
using during his stay here to retrieve a chart
he'd forgotten. By the time he reentered the
conference room, half the cookies she'd
brought were eaten and the mood was antici-
patory but relaxed.

To a person, everyone glanced up or
glanced around as LJ strode confidently to
the head of the room. Eden was certain,
however, that no one's heart raced as hers did
when LJ made eye contact.

In the nod he gave her, she searched for

something secret—a raised or lowered brow, the whisper of an un-businesslike smile, something to distinguish his greeting to her from his greeting to the others.

Lowering her eyelids and fiddling with the edge of the table, she admitted that his nod to her was disappointingly like his nod to everyone else.

Still, when he stood near her, her senses awakened like bears coming out of hibernation: they were hungry and took in everything. As always, she loved the confidently squared shoulders beneath sleek, imported fabric; the perfect, clean scent that teased her into scooting her chair closer; the hypnotic timbre of his voice.

She was ridiculously pleased that the first thing he said involved her.

"I'm glad to see you've been treated to more of Ms. Carter's excellent cookies." His smile was so full of charm and goodwill, his face so classically gorgeous she became certain his audience would agree to any plan he proposed if only she kept her mouth shut this time.

"I hope you're saving me a couple," he added, prompting Garnet Kearn to snatch two of the peanut-butter-kiss cookies and set them aside on a napkin.

"It seems," LJ continued, "that Ms. Carter's talents extend beyond baking or even being an outstanding doula. It seems she also has quite a feel for public relations."

Because it was not the opening Eden expected, she glanced up in total surprise. Seated together, Terrence and Leslie beamed at her and LJ.

"The last time we gathered in this room, Ms. Carter suggested that the first commercials my team and I came up with lacked a critical dose of realism. She proposed that new Children's Connection clients would require unvarnished candor in order to put their trust and their money into our programs. I disagreed."

LJ sounded pleasantly neutral, but Eden began to wonder where he was taking this. A peek around the table showed her that LJ's audience divided its attention between him and her. She didn't enjoy being on display in this manner, didn't like wondering what came next.

Predictability—that's what I like. She had to squelch a desire to excuse herself.

"Without belaboring the point further," LJ continued, "I'd like to show you the storyboards for a new commercial concept. A series of commercials, actually."

He unveiled a large poster board behind him. On it were handsomely drawn blocks depicting the frames of a commercial. He explained.

"Last weekend I revised the commercial's format. Rather than attractive images of a mother and child, I thought we could utilize documentary-style interviews that would allow us to ask the very questions the public needs to have answered. I wanted to impress upon the viewer that even through troubled times the clinic has continued the work of building happy families. Like a successful family, we address our issues and work through them to triumph in the end."

Eyebrows rose and heads nodded around the room. Eden saw Leslie grasp and squeeze Terrence's hand and noticed that his expression had darkened. There was no time to wonder about that, however, as LJ pressed on.

"I still thought to accomplish that objective using actors, professionals who can be relied upon to project the warmth and articulation we need to achieve our objectives. Once again, though, Ms. Carter disagreed."

Eyebrows rose higher. And all eyes beneath those hitched brows were focused on Eden.

I didn't say a word about his new commercial, she wanted to insist in defense. *I didn't even see it.* She recalled the way he'd withdrawn when he'd caught sight of the ideas she'd been working on. Was the man of her erotic dreams about to publicly castigate her for working on his campaign? Coldness seeped into her blood, her bones. Being blindsided was worse than anything.

"Eden—" LJ switched to her first name "—took the initiative to speak with a number of the clinic's clients, not as a doula, but as a peer. Based on responses to a questionnaire she conceived, she came up with her own storyboard."

For the first time since he'd begun addressing his audience, he glanced Eden's way. Again his expression remained purely professional.

"I was taken aback when I first viewed her ideas. She utilized the same basic concept I did—ask the hard questions. Give honest answers. Let the public see the real Children's Connection.

"Thankfully for all of us, Eden took the idea a crucial step further. She drew up a commercial proposal in which not only are real questions asked, but the answers are supplied by real people. Clients, legitimate clients, are interviewed rather than given lines to read. They'll be able to speak frankly about a variety of topics, including the issues that are currently affecting public opinion. We're talking about thirty- to sixty-second spots, of course, but with a series of commercials rather than one or two and with judicious directing and editing, we'll be able to address the issues efficiently."

LJ turned then to the large storyboards behind him and described a detailed mock-up of the commercial Eden had envisioned. His New York team had included dialogue culled from an interview he had obviously had with one of the couples on her "suggested contacts" sheet.

Just as clearly, he'd used her list of questions.

He'd set aside his own ego and used a layperson's ideas.

Her ideas.

As he described the commercial, she saw clearly that he and his team had turned her raw notions into something polished but utterly humane. As smiles bloomed with surprise and approval, heads nodded and the atmosphere in the room grew lighter. By the close of the presentation, coffee was being poured, the remaining cookies were attacked with gusto and she was being congratulated on a job well done as heartily as was LJ.

He made sure her efforts were acknowledged, but carefully refrained from acknowledging her himself in any personal way.

At least, she *hoped* he was carefully refraining. Because by the time the board and staff members began to drift away, she couldn't think of anything except the man who still hadn't said a word to her directly.

He had integrity. And he was humble enough to learn from someone else and to give credit where credit was due.

He had humor; he was great with Liam; he kissed as if he'd taken a college course in the subject, and if she could bottle his pheromones and take regularly scheduled sniffs she'd be on a high from now till the end of her days.

She was going to have an affair with LJ Logan.

Eden knew it now as certainly as she knew

their relationship would be a limited thing, both in the number of days it lasted and the level of emotional intimacy they would be able to achieve.

LJ held something of himself back in all situations, even when he was working the room with his gorgeous, ingratiating grin. He smiled just right, shmoozed just right: there were no rough edges; he never let down his guard.

That was okay. She didn't intend to let hers down, either.

His habit of distancing himself provided exactly the reminder she needed that he would be her Mr. Right Tonight. Their relationship would be a gift she gave herself, a memory to open whenever she wanted to in the years to come.

She didn't speak to LJ directly until he approached her with Terrence and Leslie flanking him, and then it was Terrence who said, "We can't thank you enough for participating in our little experiment, Eden. I hope your time at the coast was as enjoyable for you as it was productive for the business."

She looked at LJ. His face continued to be a mask of studied, professional politeness.

Can't have that....

Smiling at Terrence, she replied, "Absolutely. In fact, midweek there was a moment when I completely forgot we were working."

Her gaze traveled back to the deep-blue eyes that sparked with humor.

That's more like it.

"I've persuaded these two he-men to try out a new tea room with me," Leslie told her. "It's supposed to be terrific. Can we persuade you to come along?"

"Thanks, but I have to pick up Liam and head home. I have a date tonight," she confided. "My first in ages, and I want a head start getting ready. He's picking me up at six o'clock." She stared hard into LJ's eyes. "Sharp."

Chapter Eleven

By five-fifty-five, Eden had convinced herself LJ hadn't gotten the message that *he* was her hot date.

She'd dressed in a swirly skirt the color of a peach margarita, a gauzy sleeveless top the same shade and strappy tan sandals that laced around her bared-for-spring ankles. It really wasn't warm enough to wear the outfit, but her inner thermostat seemed to be set on Heat tonight.

Liberty was at the market with Liam. The ultrasupportive roommate had volunteered to babysit the moment Eden confessed she'd impulsively suggested tonight's rendezvous. She'd told Eden to stay out as late as she wanted and planned to treat Liam to an evening of Hap Palmer DVDs and herself to a really good artichoke and spinach pie from Pizza Roma.

Waiting for LJ, Eden paced in front of the window, chewing her lip and wondering whether he'd totally mistaken her message or had reconsidered and rejected the idea of getting involved with her.

She was in the bathroom, applying more of the lip gloss she'd eaten off, when the doorbell rang.

The tube of gloss clattered into the sink. Hastily retrieving and tossing it onto the vanity, she sprinted to the living room, then forced herself to slow her remaining steps to the door. Her heart hammered as, rising slightly on her toes, she angled her gaze through the peephole.

Holy date night. Her superhero had arrived.

Opening the door to LJ Logan, possibly the first and only man she had ever wanted to make love to without the attendant fantasies of forever, Eden simply stared through the screen.

Dressed in a handsome suit of midnight-blue, his hair damp around the collar from a recent and obviously hasty shower, he wore a serious expression.

Eden figured it was her duty as hostess and instigator of tonight's rendezvous to say something, but her brain was so foggy she couldn't find a thought with a flashlight.

LJ took on the task of the opening line.

"You look gorgeous. I hope to hell I understood you correctly. Because if some other guy shows up, I'm going to have to kick his ass."

Eden had made dinner reservations downtown, close to LJ's apartment. They used his cell phone to cancel.

Perfunctorily she reminded herself that she'd fallen into bed with guys in the past and had her heart broken, but that did absolutely nothing to make her resist LJ as he moved them closer and closer to the point of the evening.

They had come together to make love. He knew it; she knew it. Neither of them wanted food, and going to dinner first to increase the anticipation would have seemed akin to pouring a cup of water in the Pacific Ocean: not necessary.

They drove his car and studiously avoided touching—not even a hand to the small of the back or fingertips grazing an arm—as they entered his building and took the elevator to his apartment. It wasn't until the elevator doors opened that LJ touched her waist as she moved past him.

That's all it took. They were lip-locked while the doors tried to close.

To Eden, the kiss felt like coming home after a long, aimless walk. Somehow, with the first hungry touch of his lips she knew he was the bull's-eye for which she'd been aiming since she'd first discovered boys.

Liberty swore sex was better with a man from whom no future was expected. Maybe she was right. As LJ's lips and hands moved boldly, steadily over her, Eden knew she had never…ever…ever felt such a flood of hormones, such an urgent and utterly enlivening *need* fill her body. Blood seemed to leave her limbs and surge toward her groin.

In her youth, even when her desire to feel saved and protected had made her boy crazy, she'd never hungered to make love. She'd realized all too soon that she could feel as alone after that act of intimacy as she'd felt before it. Disappointment was the price of trading sex for hugs, and promises that would never be kept.

LJ offered no promises. From him she required none. He wanted to make love as much as any of the randy young men she had known. But he hungered for *her*—not just for sex. The obvious strength of his desire made her feel reckless and wanton and more curious about the act of love, what it would be like with him, than she'd ever been in her life.

He pulled away so they could walk to his apartment, grinning and steadying her when she swayed, clearly weak in the knees. Her mind felt weak, too. She barely noticed his opening the door, and once they were in the bedroom, she couldn't have said at all what the living-room furniture looked like or whether there was any artwork on the hall walls.

The closer they came to the bed, the more her mind began to spin.

Sorry she'd waited to talk to a doctor about birth control and not quite trusting breast-feeding as a method, she'd bought a package of condoms on the way home from work. Should she mention that or just present him with a foil packet? Briefly she wished for the old days when her birth control method required no discussion.

And suddenly she realized LJ stood before her and that they were both standing in front of his bed and that his hands were already reaching up to remove his tie.

Reaching for the hem of her gauzy top, she pulled it over her head.

Once they started disrobing, they didn't pause. Working on their own garments then reaching for each other's, they got naked with the speed of two kids shucking their clothes to go skinny-dipping. Except LJ looked nothing like a kid. Didn't act like one, either.

He circled Eden's breasts with his tongue when her bra came off…pushed her hands away so he could deal with her skirt himself…knelt before her to remove her underwear and kissed her so intimately— and exquisitely—she lost her breath. He might have meant the caress to be quick, just a small part of the play, but he grabbed her hips strongly when a moan escaped her, and despite the fact that she urged him to stand up, he remained right where he was, holding her in place, working miracles with his mouth and tongue until she felt that she was standing on the edge of a cliff with nowhere to go but over the edge.

The surprise of it stole Eden's breath as much as the incredible act itself. Other men had explored her as intimately, but she'd never been comfortable enough to lose control, never lost—and found—herself in the shuddering aftermath. LJ was good. He was so, so good.

And he wasn't done yet. Not by a long shot.

Her release urged him on. He held her hips, supporting her until her quivers subsided, but then he stood, swept her into his rock-solid arms and set her on the bed. Naked, too, he hovered over her, one knee between her legs. His face was a masterpiece of masculine lines and angles, its expression strained by lust.

"I can't slow down," he warned, his voice as tense as his body.

Because Eden couldn't yet find the breath to form words, she nodded, giving him the okay he sought, and LJ reached down to spread her legs. He hovered above her a moment, as if considering what a little self-control might cost him, but the price must have been too high. Her legs were draped over his arms, her hips raised, her heart still hammering madly from her own pleasure and from the anticipation, when he drove inside, plunging them both into an experience that felt half like madness, half like paradise.

LJ was torn between anger and euphoria. He had just experienced, without doubt, the best sex of his life. It seemed safe to assume that Eden had enjoyed herself, too, but his behavior ranked right up there with a horny bull's. He was thirty-seven. He had experience in this area; he possessed some finesse. But he hadn't shown it.

Lying under the covers in a king-size bed that was his for the rest of the month only, he wondered if Eden wanted to slug him. He'd made her skip dinner, brought her up to his rented apartment and practically attacked her.

He was the date from hell. Why had she put up with him?

Turning from his current position—on his back, staring at the ceiling lit only by the dim, warm light from the master bath—he rolled onto his right side, propped himself on his elbow and gazed at the woman lying quietly with the top sheet tucked neatly into her armpits.

"You can tell me to go to hell."

Illuminated by the soft slice of light, her brows rose. "Go to hell."

He winced, his stomach tightening so hard he thought he might be ill. How was he supposed to handle this? He was still wondering when she flipped onto her side to face him.

"Why am I saying that, exactly? I mean, I aim to please, 'cause after all *you* did, but it does seem a little kinky to tell the guy who just gave you *fabulous* sex to go to, you know—" she lowered her voice dramatically "—*h-e*-double hockey sticks."

LJ sat up all the way, unmindful of the sheet that fell a little lower than his hips. "You thought the sex was fabulous?"

She pursed her kiss-swollen lips and considered. "Okay, that might be an insufficient description. Awesome, mind-blowing, eternal. The kind of sex you definitely want to brag to your best friends about— Oh, my God." She sat up next to him, catching her portion of the sheet to cover herself. "Don't tell me. You didn't think it was mind-blowing, and now I'm going to be really embarrassed and have to think of a smooth way to get my clothes, get dressed and leave before dinner without acting like I'm devastated."

LJ slid a hand through hair so thick and blond it reminded him of the vanilla taffy he'd loved as a boy. *This is the only color hair should be,* he decided in that moment, then cupped the back of her head. "I did think it was mind-blowing. And I do not want you to leave before dinner."

Drawing her toward him and meeting her halfway, he pressed his lips to hers. Soft. Perfect. More delicious than any meal in town. He took care to kiss her slowly, even solicitously, using the control he'd forfeited earlier. She deserved—

Something stirred low in his belly.

—his very best.

He turned fully toward her, tracing her jaw, her neck, her collarbone, staying away from any area remotely construed as sexual. "Above all, please don't get your clothes."

He kissed her again, with great care, with tenderness, then said as he pulled away, "I don't want you to go anywhere. Not yet."

Supporting her, he traced designs along her upper back, her spine. He felt the shiver, pressed his lips to the curve where her neck met her shoulder and felt the gooseflesh race across her skin. "I want a chance to get this right," he murmured.

"It wasn't right the first time?"

"I want to get it *exactly* right." He trailed his fingertips like feathers down her arm and up again. "Unless you're too hungry and want dinner. We lost our first reservation, but do you have another favorite restaurant downtown?"

She half gasped, half giggled when his tongue touched her collarbone. "Pizza," she said breathlessly.

LJ lifted his head. "Pizza? I'll take you for caviar. Champagne. White chocolate truffles."

"Pizza," she said, delving her fingers into his hair and pulling him toward her.

Resisting, LJ looked at her and frowned. "How about Higgins? Their seafood is always good."

Arching up since he refused to come to

her, Eden pressed three small kisses onto his parted lips, insisting in between pecks, "Pizza...pizza... pizza."

"Eden—"

Pressing her hands to his shoulders and pushing him back against the pillows, she rolled herself on top of him in a surprise move, straddling his hips and bending low to deliver another, more lingering kiss. Rising up just a bit, she smiled and waggled her brows at him. "Pizza. They deliver."

"When you said brunch, I pictured a three-egg omelet and a mimosa, not egg salad on white bread," Ryan Logan complained to his elder brother, Jake, while he eyeballed the sandwich he'd bought from a vending machine.

"You should never use the word *brunch,* anyway." Scott Logan added his admonishment in a low tone, peering suspiciously at his own vending machine turkey and Swiss, "Unless you want us to assume you've gotten completely whipped—"

"Hey!" Jake stopped his brothers, throwing a telling glance at his two-year-olds.

LJ saw Max, one of the fraternal twins his brother Jake was adopting, stare at Scott.

"They hear *everything*," Jake warned. "Especially when you're sure they're not listening." To the boy and girl he already considered his, he said, "Uncle Scott was just saying he can't wait to go to the face painting exhibit with us. Who wants to draw on his face first?"

Glancing up from his sandwich, Ryan raised his hand. "I do."

Scott, in LJ's opinion possibly the most self-contained and serious of his three brothers, glared at Ryan and gave Jake a look of pure horror. "Like he—" Glancing at the twins, he amended, "I'll pass on the face painting, thanks."

"I don't see why," Ryan groused, opening an extra packet of mustard for the egg salad. "*I* had to play supermarket shopping spree."

LJ recalled the twins' glee as they'd loaded up kid-size baskets of plastic food items with Ryan acting as the cashier. He couldn't help but picture himself doing that with Liam someday.

He hadn't thought too much of it when Jake had suggested meeting at the Portland Children's Museum for the brothers' get-together. Ever since Jake had married Stacey Handley and accepted her twins as his own, Jake had turned into a family man through and through. Today he was giving Stacey a break from mommy duty.

Like I did with Eden, LJ thought, except that we're not married, dating or pursuing a mutually enjoyable fling. We're going to be each other's pleasant memory. End of story. Jake, on the other hand, had been in love with Stacey since high school. And vice versa. There was something about being in love with someone that made taking care of them a noble thing.

Friday night had been everything Eden had said—amazing, unreal, the kind of night you wanted to brag about. She'd been talking about the sex, but for LJ there had been other factors influencing the stellar evening.

He had never felt so...close...to anyone in all his life.

Lying in bed during the afterglow, eating pizza with Eden on the sofa, talking about her dream of living just outside the city where Liam could grow up running through fields that turned green in the spring and frosted with snow in winter, LJ had put himself in the picture she'd painted.

Not intentionally, of course. He was always a man who lived in the present when it came to relationships, and he pictured his own home in a city where snow was just something that slowed you down on your way to hailing a cab.

Eden sparked thoughts of a different future entirely, one that was planned in a king-size bed while two people held hands under the covers, touched toes and gazed at the dark ceiling as if it were a map of their dreams.

That scared him. Though not as much as it should have. Not enough to send him running.

On Saturday morning, he'd awakened without her, having dropped her at her place the night before. He'd always had relationships with women whose lives were full, so it shouldn't have surprised him when she'd said her weekend was already spoken for. Certainly he had plenty to do, too. Saturday morning, however, he'd awakened wanting her with him, wanting to make waffles.

Waffles, for crying out loud!

"What's wrong with *you?*" Taking his attention off his egg salad for a moment, Ryan noticed his eldest brother's scowl. "You look pissed. I warned you not to get the roast beef. It's a strange color. You want to trade half of yours for half my egg salad?"

Scott answered for LJ. "If the roast beef is a strange color, why do you want it?"

One hand over his heart, Ryan gestured toward LJ with the other. "He's my brother. I'm willing to sacrifice."

"No, you're not." Scott called him out. "You're still trying to score the best lunches, like you did in high school. No one's sandwich was safe."

"I'm a growing boy."

Jake, the M.D. of the family, laughed at the exchange. "You will be a growing boy if you don't slow down on the chips and cookies." He nodded toward the array of junk food in front of Ryan. "You're a bad influence on my kids."

Ella appeared at her new daddy's knee, raised her arms and requested irresistibly, "Pick me."

Jake's lips curved with a smile softer than any LJ had ever witnessed on his brother's face. "Pick you? Like a flower?" he asked as he scooped the girl up and set her on his lap. He kissed the top of her head, and Ella giggled.

Why did that simple moment put a feeling of intense pressure in LJ's chest? The beautiful child curled into Jake with utter trust. Across the table Max had pulled apart his peanut-butter-and-jam sandwich and was pressing the jam side onto his tongue in a valiant effort to eat only the sticky preserves. LJ noticed Ryan inching away from the toddler, hoping to keep his clothes safe from purple fingers, but LJ thought the boy's concentration was fascinating. He could easily picture Liam in a couple of years, doing the same thing.

There was the squeezing feeling in his chest again.

"Taking care of kids is hard, isn't it?" he demanded of Jake, who looked at him in surprise, obviously caught off guard by the intensity of the question. "I mean, it's a big, big responsibility, right?" LJ pressed. "Twenty-four/seven. Causes tremendous stress. You probably see a lot of heart attacks in people who are parents."

Jake looked at him as if he needed his head examined, not his body.

LJ held out a hand, indicating the table full of food. "Diet, for example. How do you guide kids toward a healthful diet? Do you know there are more overweight children in

America today than ever before? They watch videos and play computer games instead of exercising. Juvenile diabetes is practically an epidemic." He started to perspire as the facts he'd read pounded inside his head. "It used to be that breastfed infants fared better on the height/weight charts than their formula-fed peers, but that's changing."

Scott and Ryan stared at their big brother as if he'd sprouted a third eye.

LJ reached for his bottled water and took a swig. Okay, so he'd been on the Internet again last night. But it was true, wasn't it, that parenting was the toughest job in the world? Jake was the only one of them who had any experience. Despite growing up with the most dedicated father on the planet, the Logan brothers had, one and all, remained unencumbered into their midthirties.

Although, LJ amended mentally, Scott was only thirty. Fairly normal for a man to be single and childless at that age. Ryan, however, was thirty-six. Jake had held out until thirty-five, and he—

Pinching the bridge of his nose, he winced. At thirty-seven, he was the worst of the lot— already closing in on forty, and he had never, not ever, committed himself to a woman, much less considered parenting a child.

He had always considered his choice to remain single to be a conscientious and respectable one. So why did it suddenly make him feel puny and shallow? He looked at the twins, and he wanted to ask Jake questions about Dr. Sears, potty training, how to start a college fund and whether Jake ever worried about loving two kids who had been fathered by another man.

Then he looked at his brother kissing the top of Ella's head and even caught him taking an extra moment to inhale the scent of her silky hair, and for a second LJ felt so dizzy he thought he might black out. With the clarity of a much wiser man, he knew Jake would see no difference between the twins and his biological child, if he had one. Jake loved Stacey; the toddlers were hers. What her heart cherished, his would, too.

"Are you all right?" Scott's voice came to him as if from a distance. "LJ, what is up with you, man? Do you have a headache or are you having a spiritual experience?"

Ryan cracked, "Watching the Blazers is as close as big brother's ever come to a divine encounter. He must have a migraine. Jake, give him a painkiller."

Jake glanced up and met LJ's eyes. He grinned. "Moody? Distracted? Asking questions about kids? He's all right. I think he's just in love."

LJ felt rather than saw both Ryan and Scott stare at him, wide-eyed. As if he'd been caught hiding pictures of Heather Locklear under his pillow when he was a teenager, LJ's face started to flame.

"Holy moley. I'm right." Jake's smile softened, turned understanding. "Been there, done that myself. You planning to tell us about it?"

LJ's private affairs had always been... private, but this time he needed to talk. He'd have liked to wait until he had the chance to speak with Jake alone, but that could take a few days, and there was no way he'd make it through the weekend with the confused knot of feeling currently constricting his chest.

Not knowing how or where to begin, he blurted, "I slept with a woman last night, and when I woke up this morning I wanted to make waffles."

Ryan and Scott exchanged baffled glances.

"Waffles are good," Scott offered.

"I like the Belgian ones." Ryan nodded. "The thick kind."

"I wanted to make them with a woman!" LJ practically shouted, as if that explained his dilemma. Two tables over, a couple of mothers with a group of young kids frowned at him. Lowering his voice, leaning over the table, he hissed, "I've been thinking about her all morning."

"While you're with us?" Scott intoned.

"Yes."

"That's not very flattering," Ryan added.

Scott shook his head. "Not at all."

"Okay, Dumb and Dumber, your input is no longer required." LJ waved at the junk food. "Count your M&M's while Jake and I have an adult conversation."

He turned to Jake, a respected doctor, a man who'd traveled around the world and found his fate in his hometown. Unable to speak with anything but raw sincerity, he asked, "Help me out here. I think I'm going crazy. This is everything I've *never* wanted, and now I feel as if I can't live without it. But she's got a kid, and what if this is a passing thing for me? I don't want to hurt her."

His stomach began to churn so much he wondered whether the vending machines carried antacids. "I'd hate my own guts if I ever hurt Liam—that's her son." He shook his head. "I know he's just a baby, but you should see him. He's going to have a great personality. Fun and has a sense of humor already. And Eden—that's her name—Eden, she's..."

His heart rate accelerated. Maybe he was having a panic attack. Or a coronary. "She's smart. Compassionate. Beautiful, too, but once you get to know her there's so much more to notice."

Scott and Ryan would have been speechless even if they hadn't been ordered to stifle themselves. Jake's understanding smile turned downright commiserating, and Max raised his piece of jam-slathered bread, a hole chewed out of the middle, and smeared it onto LJ's forearm.

Jake sprang forward, ready to intervene, but changed his mind, perhaps deciding LJ needed to get used to jam in his arm hair. Cuddling Ella, he mused, "Kind of like seeing the ocean for the first time, isn't it? Beautiful. Terrifying. Completely out of your control." He offered the most reassuring smile he could. "Come on in, the water's fine."

Chapter Twelve

Early Monday morning, Eden dropped Liam off at day care, then went on three house calls before she made her way back to the clinic. Having clients to focus on was a blessing, but one woman, a forty-two-year-old first-time mother-to-be, was a Children's Connection client who had tried for ten years to become pregnant. She and her husband were ecstatic but nervous about the pregnancy. The husband routinely scheduled his work around his wife's appointments with Eden so that he could be present and supportive and completely involved in the pregnancy.

Normally Eden loved working with the devoted couple. They were excited and jittery enough to be kids, but as easy and comfortable with each other as furniture that had filled the same house for generations.

Today when the man had squeezed his wife's hand, when he'd brought up her nausea and asked for solutions because she was, in his words, "too sweet to complain," Eden had developed a bad case of flop sweat. So bad, the courteous husband and noncomplaining wife had offered to turn on the central air, make her an iced tea, call the paramedics.

Declining intervention, Eden lied by pleading bad eggs at breakfast and escaped as soon as possible thereafter.

She had spent all weekend with Liam, snuggling in her bed, watching Baby Mugs, Baby Songs, Baby Einstein, Baby-You-Name-It DVDs and sharing a box of Earth Mother Teething Biscuits. LJ had started phoning and leaving messages Saturday evening.

Eden had known on Friday night when he'd dropped her off at home that she couldn't see him again that weekend. After making love twice on Friday night, they had shared pizza in his living room. He'd told her a little bit about growing up with four brothers, how his family had ordered four pizzas at a time instead of one, how the boys had shaken each other's soda cans before they were opened and how they had once put a dead worm on a combo slice and told an unbeloved babysitter it was just an anchovy. She bit into the worm and quit that night.

By the end of the evening, Eden wanted to meet LJ's parents and all his brothers. She'd already met his brother Jake at a couple of Children's Connection social affairs, as Jake was married to Stacey Handley Logan, a social worker at the clinic. Eden didn't know him well, but after Friday night, her mind wandered continually to scenarios involving delightful family get-togethers, each one featuring LJ and his family.

Afraid she was a fraud masquerading as a self-actualized woman and advocate of single motherhood, she had known she could not see LJ again until she straightened out her thoughts. She told him she was busy

Saturday daytime, ignored his calls in the evening and spent Sunday on Sauvie Island looking at flowers and organic vegetables so she wouldn't have to listen to the phone machine.

Liberty thought she was taking a little emotion far too seriously, but because she had always maintained a safe distance in her own relationships, she honored Eden's request not to pick up the phone if LJ called. So Eden had lasted the weekend not speaking to him and hoping she could gain perspective.

She told herself that she and LJ had not "made love"; they'd had sex. Further, he was not calling because he wanted to look at vegetable starts with her; he wasn't interested in sharing her life. He was calling because the aforementioned sex had been mighty fine, and he was a guy, and so of course he wanted to see her again. When he went back to New York there would be a new woman. Or one he had known previously.

As she sank into her desk chair on Monday morning, her thoughts drained and depressed her, though she did decide it was a darn good thing she'd bought condoms, because—

Oh. Dear. God.

The condoms.

In a deep interior pocket of the slouchy shoulder bag she'd been using for the past week, there were still several foil packets—not that she'd been assuming they'd make love…have sex…that many times—but when she'd slipped the packets into her purse she'd reasoned that if she was going to be prepared, she ought to be fully prepared.

A mature and responsible decision.

Too bad she had completely, 120 percent forgotten to have that little birth control moment with LJ. He'd never said a word, either. No doubt he'd assumed she had the protection angle covered, being a doula and working at a clinic where these topics were mundane.

Slouching in her chair, she considered the past couple of days. Staying away from LJ, continuing her life as a solo mom had been a good choice. Their attraction discombobulated her. At one point on Friday night he'd spooned with her, pulling her into his body and curving around her, then sighing as though the affection was as satisfying as the sex. No wonder she'd forgotten about birth control. She forgot most everything in his arms. The defenses that had kept her safe from heartbreak for years began to crumble.

Now that she'd had two days' worth of distance from the source of temptation, she realized that breaking her abstinence from relationships had been a treacherous mistake.

Reaching for the purse she'd plunked at her feet when she'd sat down, Eden opened an exterior zippered pouch and extracted the package of peanut butter cups she'd picked up in the cafeteria on the way to her office. Not that the cafeteria was on the way to her office, but she'd been ravenous for sugar ever since she'd ordered herself to *Stop thinking about LJ Logan.*

For five seconds.

For five measly seconds.

Ripping open the package, she brought the candy to her lips, intending to take a huge mind-numbing bite, but she paused when the aroma of milk chocolate and sweetened peanut butter assailed her.

LJ smells better than chocolate. He smells like…like a cozy fire on a rainy day…like sunshine in the morning…moonglow at midnight…elm trees in autumn and—

"This," she said to the empty office, stuffing the first peanut butter cup quickly into her mouth, "is why I'm going to end the fling. End it." The sugary filling and chocolate melted together. The tension in her body began to yield to the sweetness, sending a signal to her brain to eat the other piece quickly. "That's it, affair over. Today it's peanut butter cups, tomorrow it'll be Snickers…then what? A Dove bar? If I keep seeing him, I'll be a blimp."

"Then you can fly yourself back east to visit me. Save on airfare." LJ lazed in the doorway observing her with interest. "I assume ours is the affair you're planning to end," he said, sounding quite calm. "Though I have no idea what that has to do with chocolate. Care to explain it to me?"

Never had a mouthful of her favorite candy tasted more cloying. Embarrassment surged through Eden. *Note to self: Close the damn door if you're going to scarf chocolate to numb your feelings.*

Putting serious effort into dispatching the last mouthful, she chewed and decided she was not self-actualized enough to admit that she was eating to avoid near-constant thoughts about him.

Instead, she said, once she'd swallowed, "No man can fully understand a woman's relationship to chocolate."

He waited for elaboration, his gaze less relaxed than his smile, but in the end he shrugged and pushed away from the door.

Keeping one hand behind him, he advanced until he was directly opposite her, whereupon he whipped a lovely bouquet of spring flowers from behind his back.

Eden's eyes widened involuntarily. The flowers were perfect: wild and sweet, just like—

Just like making love to him.

In the act of reaching out her hand, she jerked back.

He tilted his head inquisitively. "I did consider a box of Godiva, but passed. The last thing I want is to be blamed for the demise of a truly excellent figure." She didn't move. "Come on, Eden, they won't bite."

"I can't take the flowers." Her voice was unsteady. She was unsteady. "We need to talk."

LJ sighed. "Mind if I sit? No? Thanks." Seating himself across from her, he held the bouquet in his lap. "Shoot."

Hmm. She hadn't intended to have the discussion now, at work. With the door open.

Grabbing a tissue to wipe the chocolate off her fingers—while LJ grinned at her—she rose to shut the door, aware of his gaze as she rounded the desk. Her skin tingled and she was very conscious of the hips she'd considered a size too large since her pregnancy. On Friday, though, LJ had told her he loved her curves, that she reminded him of the great screen sirens. She'd never felt so sexy.

Or cherished.

Or filled with mindless desire.

Which was the problem. Because when a person was as mindlessly desirous as Eden, lives could be altered. Hearts could be broken.

Striding with businesslike efficiency to her chair, she sat with a back so straight any nun who'd ever wielded a ruler would be proud. Folding her hands atop the desk, she made direct eye contact. No dithering.

LJ noted her crisp body language with bemused surprise. Shrugging, he laid the flowers aside, sat forward in his chair and clasped his hands atop the desk, as well. If you can't beat 'em...

He's trying to be humorous, Eden

thought. Serious discussions probably unnerve him. It made sense; he was a thirty-seven-year-old bachelor who didn't want commitment. He'd rather keep his conversations with women light.

Briefly she considered shelving today's topic, but it formed the basis of her thesis, *Why Eden And LJ Must Break Up*.

"We have a problem," she stated. "It's about Friday."

He nodded. "I sorta figured that. What's the problem?"

"I haven't been on birth control since well before I conceived Liam. And there hasn't been any need since then."

He jerked a little. Yeah, she'd gotten his attention.

"I began to think seriously about birth control on Friday after I made the date with you."

She saw LJ relax a little.

"I bought a box of condoms."

He nodded, smiled his approval. And then he understood. "We didn't..."

"No, we didn't." She waited for that to sink in all the way. "I never even thought of it again until this weekend. And I take much of the responsibility for this, because you probably thought I was on something. Although, we certainly should have had that discussion. Also, we didn't even consider STDs—"

"I don't have an STD!"

"Well, neither do I! But it's something we should have discussed." He was scowling now, looking almost as disgusted with himself as she felt. "At least we both agree that we behaved irresponsibly."

He nodded.

"And that it can't happen again."

He considered this. "Absolutely. I trust your word, but I'm very willing to take a blood test, so you won't waste energy worrying. Fortunately, we're working in a hospital and one of my brothers is a doctor, so it shouldn't take too long."

"What? No!"

"No?"

"No. If you say you don't have— I mean STDs weren't my point, really. We weren't thinking—that's the point. We were so *not thinking* that we let ourselves act like kids with raging hormones."

LJ grimaced. "You're really focused on

hormones. I suppose that makes sense, given your job. Still, I can assure you that what happened Friday night was not all about hormones."

The hot, hot, superhot expression in his eyes not only made her lose her train of thought, it nearly propelled her over the desk to see if they could rekindle some of Friday night's fire. She had to sift through her mixed-up thoughts like a miner trying to find a nugget of something worthwhile.

"I was referring to the fact that we…that I…" She shook her head. Why wasn't he getting this? "I'm talking about the pregnancy angle."

LJ sat straighter. "I forgot about the pregnancy possibility." His impatience with the conversation eased, but he frowned and shook his head. "A baby. Becoming pregnant again so soon after having Liam would be rough for you, wouldn't it? Did you have any problems with your first pregnancy?"

His response, so unlike any she'd expected, threw her for a loop. Mystified, she stood. "What does my first pregnancy have to do with anything? You're missing the point. What's important here is that you and I…we're the wrong people. We're ships that pass in the night. Fireworks that explode and then—" she waved her hands "—*pfft!*"

"'*Pfft*'?"

"Fizzle. People who are going to fizzle have no business engaging in unprotected sex." She looked at him darkly and said once again, "We weren't thinking, because we're too attracted."

"Too attracted?"

"To each other."

"That part was kind of implied. Let me see if I'm following you. It's your opinion that you and I are too attracted to each other, which led to spontaneous and unprotected sex, which is proof that…" He frowned. "This is where I get confused."

"It's proof that we're the right people at the wrong time. Or no, the wrong people at the right—" She shook her head, confusing herself. "No, we're the wrong people at the wrong time. It's just wrong. We can't have sex again. It could be a disaster. I'm fairly certain this is a safe time for me, but breast-feeding a baby makes it difficult to tell."

"I read that breastfeeding is a pretty good birth control method in itself."

"It's not foolproof."

"I'd be interested in learning more about that."

"Have you hit your head? Do you understand what I'm telling you? We…didn't… use…birth…control. Imagine yourself in nine months as a daddy."

She waited for the reaction. He continued to gaze up at her without standing. *Probably can't,* she thought. *If it's starting to sink in, he's probably gone numb from the waist down.* Which was good, because he needed to understand the enormity of what they'd done. No one should chance becoming a parent when he wasn't ready to accept all of the consequences. Family was "for better or worse," and when people didn't accept that, when they abandoned ship during the "for worse," it was devastating.

And yet all he said when he finally spoke was, "I'm not worried about it."

Liar. "If you're not worried, then why are you sweating?" She pointed to his forehead.

LJ reached up and felt the thin sheen of moisture. His lips did that attractive ironic twist that reminded her of Harrison Ford and George Clooney and Clark Gable. "Okay,

I'm a *little* worried. You, however, seem highly agitated, so let's concentrate on calming you down."

Now he rose and came around to her side of the desk. His hands settled on her shoulders to massage away the tension. Eden jumped back as if his touch were fire rather than the warm, gentle-yet-firm caress she'd been dreaming about all bloody weekend long.

"Who are you, and what have you done with LJ Logan?" She practically yelped the question. He was scaring the stuffing out of her. This was not the man with whom she'd begun a casual, no-strings, no-commitment, no-how, no-way fling. A man who hadn't known the first thing about kids just a couple weeks ago and hadn't seemed to care. And, moreover, a man who at thirty-seven had never been married, because he'd never wanted to be.

LJ took a step forward. A small smile remained on his lips, but his gaze was so focused, so intent he looked almost dangerous. "Do you think I'd run from a responsibility that important, that profound, Eden? Do I seem like a man who doesn't think his actions through very carefully?"

He was still advancing. Eden was still backing up.

"Not using birth control was an aberration, I admit." He spoke calmly and deliberately. "But, let's not confuse *aberration* with *tragedy*. If you got pregnant, I would stand beside you." He caught up with her to cup the back of her neck this time, where his fingers resumed the attempt to soothe her rattled nerves. "Correction—I would stand *with* you. If we did it together—you, me and Liam—how awful would it be, Eden?"

Okay, now she knew what was wrong: she'd hit her head and was imagining the conversation. Probably had slipped into unconsciousness smack in the middle of her fave fantasy—the one in which LJ promised fidelity and swore to be there for her and Liam forever and ever, amen. She'd be crushed when she woke up and Prince Charming turned out to be a man with a commitment phobia.

Don't get sucked in, Eden, don't get sucked in, don't get sucked in....

"Whatever is going on in that busy, beautiful head of yours, would you please fill me in?"

She reached up to remove his hand from the nape of her apparently highly sensitive neck so she could think more clearly. LJ curled his fingers around hers, refusing to allow retreat.

"Talk to me," he insisted. "We made love. Some straight conversation shouldn't be much of a stretch."

His choice of words was unnerving. They weren't supposed to have been "making love." They were supposed to have been having sex. Emotions need not apply.

"Okay, straight up. On Friday night we both knew that whatever was going on between us would have a shelf life," she said. "You live in New York, for one thing. I live in Oregon. You're not moving. I'm not moving. That alone makes a relationship impossible."

"Nothing is impossible." He spoke quietly. Assuredly. As if he'd thought about this. "I like New York. My business is there. But New York isn't the only state that needs public relations experts. I'm working in Portland right now, aren't I?"

When hope seemed to replace the blood pumping through her veins, Eden quashed it.

A possible explanation for his change of

heart occurred to her. "You've spent a lot of time lately talking to families with children, reading about women who want a baby more than anything. And you've spent just enough time with Liam to be seduced by the cuddling and cuteness without having to suffer through sleepless nights or endless crying for no apparent reason or the manic-depressive toddler years. I think you have baby fever."

"I have a fever, but not the one you've diagnosed, Doc."

LJ had reached the edge of her desk while she'd continued to back up to the bookcase. Recognizing that the only place left for her to go was through the wall, he'd stopped moving forward. Now he leaned a hip against her desk and considered her thoughtfully.

"My brother Jake was a dedicated bachelor. No one thought he'd get married, at least no one I know. Now he's married to Stacey, adopting her twins, and he's happier than I've ever seen him. In fact, maybe he's happy for the first time."

Eden's tongue felt as if someone had run a vacuum over it. Her heart beat harder than it ever had. "What are you saying? You want to be like Jake?"

"No, I want to be like me. With you. What happened between us Friday isn't something I take for granted. I'm not talking about just sex, either, so don't go there. I'm talking about what happened after the sex."

"What happened afterward? We had pizza."

His eyes glinted appreciatively. "You're going to keep me on my toes, aren't you? I'm talking about the next morning. I wanted you to be there." Stepping away from the desk, he allowed his straightforward posture to reflect the seriousness of his words. "In my bed. And at the breakfast table. I thought about you all weekend." He stepped forward slowly, a hand out as if to steady her, the way he would a frightened deer. "Did you think about me, too?"

She swallowed with difficulty, nodded then raised both of her hands as he tried to touch her cheek. "Don't touch me yet. I need to be able to think."

The fire that flashed in his eyes said he understood her meaning: she simply couldn't think straight, couldn't concentrate on anything but him—them—when any part of them was making contact. Nodding slightly he lowered his arm.

Eden rushed to speak before she lost her nerve. "We had two different experiences this weekend. Yes, I thought of you, too. I thought about what a future would be like if we had something ongoing. I didn't like thinking about it so much, LJ. I made a decision to be a single parent because—" A rush of grief caught her off guard. Tears stung her eyes.

"Talk to me."

She wasn't sure if he spoke out loud or whether she heard his voice in her head—soft, compelling.

"From the age of ten to when I was seventeen, my life was a wreck. And it was a wreck, because my mother couldn't function after a man left us."

"Your father?"

"My stepfather. My father didn't stay long enough for me to remember him. And don't look at me like that."

"Like what?"

"Like you've got me figured out now. I've been to therapy. I've read the books. I understand all the classic abandonment issues. It's not that."

"What is it?"

"The burden of a breakup falls on the child. It just does. And I won't do that to Liam." She felt herself growing more convicted with each word. "You and I don't know each other. You've never been married, never wanted to be if I've understood you correctly up to now. You have no way of knowing if you want to be a father in the long-term, especially to someone else's son. Breaking up with a woman if things don't work out is very different from breaking up with a child."

LJ listened to her words, let them sink in. "You think I'll be careless with Liam?"

"I don't know. I'm saying that I won't be. For sure." On a deep breath she delivered the final blow. "When it comes to Liam, you're not a risk I can take."

LJ's features changed. Hardened. Tension fired the night air while he processed her conviction. He didn't try to touch her again, but by the time he spoke, his frown had been replaced by a resigned smile.

"You're right, of course. My parents raised

me to believe that nothing is more important than family, which is probably why I've remained single as long as I have. I've never wanted to risk screwing it up. Of course, Liam is still a baby. We could buy ourselves a little time to see if I have the stuff fathers are made of and whether you'd even want me to apply for the job. Who knows? You may find that the spark fizzles long before we get to the 'as long as we both shall live' phase."

"*You* could find that the spark fizzles before then."

He shrugged. "I could."

That might have made sense under other circumstances and if she were a different woman. But a fear lurked inside Eden, one she had never shared with anyone and which she could hardly bear to examine. So she ignored the voice that implored her to agree with him and allied with the one that urged, *Run*.

Shaking her head, she clung tight to the reason that made sense. To her. "You're ignoring the biggest problem. We got carried away once already. The physical attraction is too strong an influence. It's muddying the waters. The longer we stay together the more complicated it will become. I'm not good at casual anything, LJ. I never have been. I've just pretended from time to time. It was a mistake to think I could have an affair without losing myself in it. It's not going to work between us."

LJ stared a long, long time. Finally he answered softly, "Words can't win that argument."

"I'm so sorry that I mislead you."

"You didn't. Not really." He turned to pick up the flowers. Looking at them, he forced a philosophical shrug. "Maybe you're right. Maybe the attraction between us has clouded other more important issues." He held out the bouquet. "Take these anyway, all right? They're Oregon wildflowers. They suit you."

Casting her gaze toward the bouquet, hoping to hide the tears that gathered in her eyes, she raised the flowers to her nose and inhaled.

"This is exactly how I want to remember you." His voice held the edginess of multiple emotions. "Beautiful and honest. And strong enough to do what you believe is the right thing."

Honest and strong. Shame welled inside her. She was neither. "You're not angry?"

"How can I be? You're protecting your child."

Eden's stomach burned. *But not from you,* she longed to admit. *Not really from you.*

Moving to the door, he placed a hand on the knob. "I suppose we'll stick to friendship from here on in. And I hope a good business relationship?"

"Yes." The word caught in her throat. "Absolutely."

"You're a sensible woman." Nodding, he started through the door, paused and looked around again. "Just one thing, Eden. Keep me posted on whether or not we're pregnant."

Chapter Thirteen

At five-thirty that evening, LJ showed up at the day care center just after Eden arrived to pick up Liam.

Stacey Handley Logan was also present picking up her twins, Ella and Max.

"How's my favorite sister-in-law?" LJ shared a hug with the lovely blonde while Eden stood awkwardly nearby, putting her name and the time on a sign-out sheet.

"Is this the part where I point out that I'm your only sister-in-law?" Stacey laughed, blue eyes dancing.

Her eyes always look happy now, Eden

mused, well aware that for Stacey and LJ's brother Jake, marriage seemed to have a positive affect. For the time being, anyway.

LJ smiled and chatted with Stacey, showing little of the intense awareness or discomfort that Eden felt. Her schedule had continued to be fast paced; she'd had precious little time to spend thinking about him. Not that lack of time had stopped her. From the moment he'd left her office to now, she'd obsessed about his parting request: keep him informed about a possible pregnancy.

She was sure they'd had sex during the safe part of her cycle, but as she'd told him, nothing was foolproof, especially when a woman's hormones were less reliable than usual.

All afternoon Eden had had visions of herself pregnant again, so soon after Liam, and of having to tell LJ, having him either bolt for New York or "do the right thing" by offering to stay involved with her for the baby's sake. Both possibilities had made her more nauseous than morning sickness ever had.

Then there was the scenario in which she told him she was pregnant and he whooped for joy, got down on one knee and pulled out a ring he'd been carrying around, hoping for the opportunity to bring it out.

Occasionally throughout the day—say, every five minutes—she had been unable to intercept that fantasy and had, in fact, indulged in it only moments before, when she saw LJ walk into the day care center.

Now she tried—and failed utterly—not to stare as he squeezed Stacey's shoulders before squatting down to speak with her toddler son. "Hello, Max. Good to see you again."

Max, whom Eden had occasionally observed acting shy and a tad clingy with his mama, had no trouble looking LJ in the eye. "Where'th your muthstath?" he demanded in toddler-ese, making all the *s*'s sound like *th*'s. "You wipe it off?"

Stacey laughed. "Honey, Uncle LJ doesn't wear a mustache."

"Uh-huh." Max nodded broadly.

"He's right," LJ verified. "I had one Saturday. I grew it at the Children's Museum. Or I should say, Ella grew it for me. Didn't she, Max?"

"She drawed it."

LJ winked up at Stacey. And glanced over

to smile at Eden, too. "They have a face painting station at the museum," he explained. "Ella gave me a mustache. In pink."

Stacey laughed. Eden gaped.

"Where is your sister?" LJ asked the little boy who was at present manually investigating the area above his uncle's upper lip.

When Max proved too busy to answer, Stacey obliged. "My daughter is far too busy creating works of art to greet me in the doorway. Jake's the only one who rates that reception these days."

Tousling Max's hair, LJ rose.

"Are you here to accept a dinner invitation?" Stacey inquired of her bro-in-law. "Did Jake tell you I'm channeling Betty Crocker and making a layer cake for dessert?"

"No, he didn't. But I may have to crash your evening now."

"No crash required. You're invited."

"Sounds great."

Sounds great? LJ had spent part of his weekend at the Children's Museum and now he was going to eat dinner with two toddlers? Eden tried to make this picture fit with the mental image she still carried of the day they'd first met.

She listened to Stacey and him discussing the details—whether he could bring anything and what time to arrive—all the commonplace minutiae of going to a relative's house, and to her horror, she felt tears welling up. Quickly she slipped away to get Liam.

After a brief check-in with the caretaker on duty in the baby room, Eden gathered her son and cuddled him close, forcing herself to acknowledge she was envious of Stacey. The other woman had opened her life to a new love and had wound up with a family.

Family. It wasn't a numbers game, but sometimes it felt that way. Sometimes it was just plain hard to get festive with only her and Liam at the dinner table.

"Hey, where'd you go?" LJ caught up with her at the wall of individual cubbyholes provided for each child. "I didn't actually come here to see Stacey," he confided. "I want to discuss something with you. Hey, mister!" Without hesitation, he reached for Liam, who went happily into his arms while Eden collected the diaper bag she packed every morning.

"Gotta get a move on." She gave him a big fake smile. "We have dinner plans." Frozen low-fat pizza for her, strained green beans and carrots for Liam. Mmm-mmm. "So you're having dinner with toddlers. That's got to be a far cry from a night on the town in New York. Are you okay with it?"

"I'm more than 'okay' with it," he said, supporting Liam with a hand beneath the bottom, the baby's back nestled against his chest. From that vantage point, Liam grinned at his mama. "Stacey is my first sister-in-law. Up to now, a dinner with one of my brothers consisted of pizza and beer or a restaurant meal, and I've eaten more than enough of those."

"Oh."

Giving Liam soft bounces, LJ peered at her. "You all right?"

"Me? Yes." He actually *wanted* to be part of a meal involving the table manners of twin two-year-olds? The nerve of him: he kept foiling her attempts to pigeonhole him.

"I've never asked you," he said. "Do you cook?"

"I took a whole foods cooking class. I flunked brown rice sushi. Anyway, I haven't had much time lately to prepare a meal from scratch. Do you cook?"

"Not a string bean. Good thing we decided not to become an item. We'd have starved." He sounded affable, resigned to what was, not nearly as nuts and conflicted as she felt.

Eden nodded. "Good thing."

Keeping Liam in his arms, he suggested, "If you're heading for your car, I'll walk you there and we can talk on the way. I've got a business proposition for you."

"Oh." Surprised, she agreed, and they headed to a bank of elevators, one of which led to an underground parking structure. LJ got down to business while they were waiting for the elevator car to arrive.

"Your plan to use real clients in the commercials was a big hit with everyone on the board."

"That's nice."

"If you were a professional, they'd be calling you the Next Big Thing by now. My crew in New York is working on new copy based on your idea. We should be ready to shoot a couple of spots with a local production company sometime next week."

"That soon? Wow, you move fast."

He ducked his head. "In business, that can be a good thing."

His sheepishness pinched her heart. "I moved quickly, too. It was mutual. Obviously."

"I'm glad you don't blame me, Eden."

"No! I mean, there's nothing to blame."

He nodded. "Good."

The elevators doors opened and they stepped into the otherwise empty car.

"So, back to business," he said easily enough. "The board has requested—and I agree—that you be the first subject of the new series of commercials."

"Either the elevator just dropped or my stomach did. You're suggesting that I appear in the commercials? LJ, I am not an actress."

"Exactly. Wasn't that your protest from day one? No actresses need apply. If you're concerned about being nervous, don't be. The spots will be shot in a casual interview style. We'll work with a small crew, comfortable set. No pressure."

"But I have a job. Even if I wanted to—and, really, I don't—I can't take the time."

"We'll work around your schedule. And Terrence is committed to doing everything possible to facilitate this. He and Leslie both said they'll feel reassured if you're the first client up at bat. They trust you to be honest and forthcoming, and your manner is naturally appealing."

"To you maybe," she said before she realized how that sounded and blushed.

"That goes without saying," LJ agreed smoothly. "Think about it overnight, Eden. But don't think too hard. It's far less intimidating than it sounds, and it won't take longer than half a day."

The elevator deposited them at the parking structure. LJ took the lead. "Which way is your car?"

"Left and other side of the lot."

"That's too far to walk without an escort when it's dark out. Where are the security guards?"

"There are two very attentive security guards, actually. I've always felt safe here."

He scanned the parking lot, expression disgruntled until he saw one of the armed guards chatting with a woman standing near her SUV. "Huh. I wonder if there was a problem over there?"

This time the murmured concern drew a smile from Eden. "You live in New York City, and you're worried about a parking lot in Portland with not one, but two security guards?"

He kept his gaze on the guard speaking to the SUV owner. "I'm worried about *you* in a parking lot."

When they reached her car, LJ waited for her to unlock the door then took the initiative of settling Liam into the car seat on his own. He emerged bragging, "I'm getting pretty good at that."

"You are." Feeling jittery, she babbled a bit. "Of course the problem with car seats is that you finally figure out all the buckles and snaps and then you don't need them anymore."

"Maybe you will. Need a car seat again, I mean. You may have another child."

He hadn't been referring to their birth control lapse, but that was certainly where both their minds traveled.

"Someday," he added gently.

"Yeah, maybe someday."

"So in the interim, while you've still got a lot of free time on your hands—" he grinned to let her know he understood the time constraints of her working-mom's schedule "—how about doing the commercial?"

"Oh, no. Really—"

"The Children's Connection needs this, Eden. They need you. Trust me when I say that your beauty will be an asset to this campaign. We're all in agreement now that it would be wrong to use an actress," he added before she could protest, "but I know this business. A gorgeous woman filling the screen draws attention. It's a fact of life, one we're fortunate enough to be able to use to our advantage."

Eden knew for a fact she wasn't beautiful. Attractive, pretty, but no one had ever described her as gorgeous. And it certainly didn't matter. What mattered to her was that LJ had used that word. His eyes were biased. Sweetly biased.

"There's not much left I can do for the clinic," he said. "Whether it survives the slings and arrows now will depend largely on the campaign."

It wasn't the guilt trip—although that was pretty effective—that ultimately made Eden agree. It was the desire to live up to the look in LJ's eyes.

The day of the commercial shoot, Eden wasn't sure whether LJ was still in town.

She hadn't seen him in the clinic for a couple of days, and he'd said his work was pretty well finished now that the commercials were planned and plotted. A costume designer had contacted her to discuss wardrobe, and a production manager had been in touch regarding time and location and the fact she'd be paid "SAG scale," which was apparently a really ridiculous amount of money for half a day's work.

When she walked onto the "set"—in reality the living room of an exquisite rented home on tree-lined NW Ainsworth—Eden started to feel nervous. Her stomach was too queasy to eat any of the breakfast that had been set out for the crew and the cast, which today consisted of her and an interviewer, who would ask her questions she was expected to answer with as much candor and personality as she could. The interviewer would remain off camera. Only Eden's responses would be edited for the final cut.

The production assistant greeted Eden shortly after her arrival, acquainting her with the craft services table, where drinks and food would be consistently available, and with the wardrobe and makeup stylists, who were ready and waiting for her.

After declining breakfast but accepting a cup of peppermint tea to settle her stomach, Eden tried on several outfits for the wardrobe consultant. Choosing a tan skirt and a blouse in shell pink, the costumer sent her to a middle-aged woman named Kim, who made Eden feel positively pampered while she styled her hair and applied makeup in attractive earth tones.

"I'm afraid to breathe," Eden said when the process was complete. Turning her head from side to side, she laughed at her image in the mirror. "It's me, only better. *Much* better."

Kim laughed with her. "I was told to get you camera ready, but not to overwhelm your natural beauty." She put her head close to Eden's and looked in the mirror with her. "I think we did very well."

Eden watched her cheeks redden beneath the makeup. Oh, how she wanted to ask whether LJ had given that directive, but she didn't even know whether he was still in town. If he wasn't, would she ever see him again? Speak to him? She'd ended the relationship so soon after it had begun that certainly she had no reason to complain if he'd left town without saying "So long."

When Eden met the director, she felt her nervousness increase another notch. Like the others, though, Jeff Kasey seemed dedicated to putting her at ease.

"We're set up in the study," he told her, guiding her to a handsome room that boasted a wood-burning fireplace topped by a stunning mantel and walls lined with books. A love seat and a tall potted plant seemed to have been repositioned for the shoot and a large inviting armchair sat opposite the sofa at an angle that kept it out of camera range.

The director led Eden to the sofa and told her to relax while the lighting and sound people checked levels.

Relaxing when she was the focus of so much attention seemed impossible, however, and she began to wish she hadn't said yes to this cockamamie plan. Either that, or she should have asked Liberty to come with her. She needed moral support, someone who would love her even if her voice emerged as a croak, and she squinted from the lights and stuttered all her responses.

"Okay. We're ready to get the ball rolling." Jeff rubbed his hands together. Sitting next to Eden on the love seat, he told her, "When you're asked a question don't worry about whether your answer will work for the commercial. Answer in a way that's comfortable for you. We'll take care of editing what you give us down to a sixty-second spot and probably also a thirty-second spot." When her brows rose, he laughed. "You don't have to think about any of that. Just speak from your heart and don't worry about the results."

"Okay. Who's going to be the interviewer?"

"Hey, I hope you didn't start without me."

Both Eden and Jeff glanced up when they heard LJ Logan's jovial voice. Only Jeff showed no surprise.

"Not likely," he said, rising. "You're the boss."

LJ grinned and clapped Jeff on the back. "Don't you forget it." Of Eden, he inquired, "Are they treating you right?"

She was so shiveringly happy to see him and so surprised to hear he was the boss that all she managed was a nod.

"Did you get something to eat?"

She shook her head.

LJ mock glared at Jeff. "It figures. Workaholics like you are why we need unions."

Unruffled, Jeff responded, "Last I heard, you were still type A."

"I feed people."

"That's why you'll never be the success I am."

"Oh, but Jeff did try to feed me," Eden insisted. "So did the production assistant and the makeup artist. I'm a little too nervous to eat, that's all."

Jeff crossed his arms. "There, see? She likes me."

"Hunger is making her delirious." LJ held out a hand to Eden and pulled her to her feet. "You'll feel better with something in your stomach. Let's see what craft services put together."

"Yeah, don't mind me," Jeff called as LJ led Eden away, "I have plenty to do. I haven't had time for breakfast. You might want to bring me back a Twinkie."

LJ laughed. Lightly holding Eden's arm, he guided her to a covered patio with ice chests and a table topped with more food than a small group of people could consume in one day.

"I'm really not hungry," Eden protested

quietly, "And Jeff honestly did offer me food this morning."

"I know. I trust him. That's why he's here."

While LJ perused the items on the table, Eden allowed herself a lingering look at him. Clad in one of his perfectly tailored suits, he was handsome as usual, but that didn't account for the glad leap of her heart. She'd wished for a friend, someone who cared about her feelings, and now he was here.

"So you're the boss?" she asked while he chose a banana, a muffin and a granola bar.

"Children's Connection is the boss. I suppose you could say I'm representing the boss. How about a bagel?"

"But you knew Jeff before this?"

"He's a good friend from high school. We used to make movies together."

"Movies? You made movies?"

"Backyard videos. Kid stuff." LJ hunted for cream cheese. "We entered a couple of festivals and did okay. The bug bit Jeff, but not me."

"The bug?"

"Filmmaking. He's made a good business for himself shooting commercials, industrials, a few music videos. And he still has a feature film up his sleeve. You can't be in this business without loving it, and he does. Do you see the cream cheese?"

"I don't want cream cheese." She looked at the growing pile of food. "I can't possibly eat all that. I could barely drink my tea this morning."

"You're that nervous?"

"I'm afraid so."

He took her hand. "Come on."

Around the side of the house and through a gate was a garden with a lovely stone bench positioned beneath a maple tree.

"I saw this when we were scouting locations for the commercial." With both hands on her shoulders, LJ pressed her gently onto the bench. Maintaining contact with one hand, he stepped behind her and began to knead her shoulders.

Eden protested, feeling like a prima donna. "Everyone is waiting for me. You don't have to—"

"Shh. Ten minutes won't kill anyone. I got you into this, I'll help you get through it." He manipulated her shoulders to loosen them up then worked in toward her neck. "This is a great house, isn't it?"

"Yes, it is." Eden's head lolled from side to side beneath LJ's firm touch.

"I like this part of town. Close to Washington Park, the zoo, the Children's Museum."

"All the hot spots," Eden agreed, beginning to feel almost languid. "Visit the zoo and the Children's Museum often, do you? When you're in town, I mean."

She intended the question to be facetious, but LJ answered sincerely. "I will now that I have a young niece and nephew. I'm sure more kids will join them soon. Stacey and Jake are already discussing adding to the family. My brother was the classic bachelor before he returned to Portland. Now he's in contention for Father of the Year."

"You sound surprised."

"I am. I didn't know it could happen that way—suddenly but profoundly. Our parents are thrilled. They adore kids and were afraid neither my brothers nor I would ever give them grandchildren to spoil."

"Well, now that Jake's done it the rest of you can relax."

"Mmm-hmm." LJ rubbed more deeply into the muscles of her neck. Eden closed her eyes.

"You need to take better care of yourself,"

he said. "Your muscles are tight, you're not eating…. That's a recipe for illness. Then who would take care of Liam?"

Who *would* take care of Liam if she became ill or, heaven forbid, was in an accident? That was a question that had plagued her. She didn't have an answer yet.

"So where did you say your mother lives?" He interrupted her thoughts and immediately her shoulders stiffened again. "Not a good topic?"

"My mother's a fine topic," Eden insisted, but she heard the defensiveness in her voice. "She's just not in grandmother mode. My mom is an artist in Santa Fe."

"Career oriented?"

Eden made a noncommittal sound. She supposed Gwen was career oriented now, but she looked at her mother's artwork as being therapeutic, as well as lucrative. Gwen's work helped keep her stable. The manic depression that wreaked havoc on Eden's childhood was under control via lifestyle and alternative-healing choices that Gwen committed to with all her might.

Eden admired her mother the way she'd eventually fought back from an illness that had proven resistant to medication. It took consistent work to heal from a mental illness without the benefit of allopathic medicine.

"Do you miss having family nearby?" LJ asked.

Eden's mother discussed her struggles with mental illness freely. She spoke at women's groups; she gave interviews in art magazines and never shied away from the topic. For Eden, though, the pain of that time in her life, the way it had robbed her of her childhood and filled her with yearnings that were too deep, too intense to fulfill, kept her silent on the issue. It was private; it was hurtful.

Because she wanted to skirt this discussion, she answered scantily. "Some. How about you?"

He gave her a speculative look, aware she didn't want to discuss her life. "I've lived away from my family for years. Visits have always sufficed, but lately I wonder." Turning her around, he worked his knuckles down her spine.

"That feels good. What do you wonder?"

"Whether an uncle can be effective so many miles away."

Taken aback, she twisted around to look at him. "Will that bother you so much—if you can't be 'effective' as an uncle?"

"Yes, it will. I'm learning from experience that relationships won't wait forever."

"Your father's son?" she asked. Fascinated as she was by psychology and spiritual matters, especially as they related to family, she'd read his father's best-selling book when she was in college.

"Even my father hasn't been able to live up to his ideal 100 percent of the time, Eden. With his kids, perhaps. But he and Terrence had a falling out and have spent years each pretending the other doesn't exist."

"Your father must have tried to heal the rift. His books are all about putting relationships first. I love what he writes."

"He's contacted Terrence once or twice through the years, yes. But he won't press the issue. And his people skills seem to rust where Terrence is concerned. If he's not careful, he could go to his grave—or see Terrence go to his—still estranged."

Eden shuddered, surprised and disturbed by the revelation. "That's terrifying. If a man who built his career around relationships can't go the extra mile, what hope is there for the rest of us?"

"Plenty if we learn from his mistakes."

She shook her head. "No wonder most marriages fail."

On a laugh, LJ admonished, "Cynic."

"I'm not a cynic! I'm realistic. You said it yourself—your father's ideals evaporated when he came up against a problem with his brother."

"He's human. And he's not dead yet, Eden," LJ said wryly. "He can change."

"Do you really believe he will? You said it's been years. How many?"

LJ shook his head, looking suddenly as if he'd swallowed bitters. "How can you stay on your own path when you're always looking to the left and right?"

It was a good question. "I'm a defensive driver," she muttered.

He came around to her side of the bench. "This is your life you're joking about."

"I'm not joking."

She understood that he was telling her in a roundabout way to give them another chance, to take each day as it came instead of looking for guarantees. But he'd grown up in a stable home. He had no idea how dangerous it could be to ignore the odds. Or to overlook the writing on the wall.

Gently she asked, "LJ, how many commitments have you made—and kept—to people outside your immediate family?"

She saw his jaw clench. "Zero," he admitted.

She nodded, glad for the honesty, and decided to disclose information about Gwen whether she wanted to or not. A glimpse into her chaotic early years would be the best way to help him understand her determination not to entwine their lives emotionally.

"My mother's bipolar disorder kicked in heavily around the time I was ten. That's why my stepfather left. It was more than he could handle, and of course I wasn't his child, so when he took off that was pretty much the last we saw of him."

Eden began to look slightly to the right of LJ, not wanting to maintain eye contact anymore. His gaze felt too probing, and the truth of her past still felt somehow dark and embarrassing. "My mom, Gwen, was an artist, fairly well-known, but she couldn't concentrate enough to work or to take care of a child. There was no one to pick up the slack."

"Who took care of you?"

"I took care of myself. And of her. So, yes, I've worried about what would happen if for any reason I couldn't handle parenthood on my own. I never, never want my choices or my problems to burden my child."

"Not every man leaves." LJ sounded raw and angry. "Not every man bails out when life gets tough."

"Maybe not, but there are no guarantees."

"Of course there aren't. Do sperm donors come with a guarantee?"

The moment he said it, he was sorry. She could see the regret written on his face. Still, she answered.

"No. No one comes with a guarantee. That's my point. It's damned difficult to juggle visitation and child support and messy feelings. I've seen it among my friends over and over. In the best-case scenario when there's a breakup, all parties mean well, but a few months into it they're fighting over something, and resentments run high, and before you know it someone bails. Not always physically, but you can tell when someone doesn't want to be there. That's almost worse."

"You're going to base the rest of your life on other people's inadequacies?"

"I'm going to make decisions based on experience and knowing myself. Knowing what I can and cannot tolerate. You live in New York, LJ. I'm not going to fly out with my eight-month-old son on weekends so we can grab dinner and see if we're still compatible. Are you going to fly out here? No, don't answer that! Meeting on weekends doesn't give a couple enough information about each other, anyway."

"No, not for a girl who likes guarantees." The desire to say more trembled on LJ's lips. He resisted it, shoving a hand through his hair. "You want a bagel? The one thing I *can* guarantee is that you'll regret it if you don't eat before we start shooting."

It took a moment for Eden to realize he was really dropping the subject. "Okay."

More subdued, they returned to the craft services table, selected food and made their way back to the set. When Jeff announced they were ready to begin, LJ sat across from her and asked his questions politely. She answered just as politely. Jeff stopped them three times to encourage her to put a little more energy into her responses.

But Eden felt drained by her fear over taking a chance on LJ and exhausted by her guilt. Was she wise or was she a weakling?

When the shoot ended LJ, ever charming, thanked everyone, told Jeff he'd look at the rough cut when it was ready and left with only a brief goodbye for her.

She drove to the Children's Connection, picked up her son and headed home, where the house felt empty even though Liberty was in the living room discussing Hypno-Birthing with three friends from school.

Grabbing an iced tea and an apple, Eden headed to her bedroom to play with Liam until he fell asleep. Her favorite time of night, those minutes when she could read a book or sit with her thoughts until sleep overtook her, ticked by with agonizing slowness. Ignoring isolation was easier when she had nothing else to compare it to.

Chapter Fourteen

Four days after the shoot, LJ returned to New York. He'd left the commercial in good hands and had done all he could for his uncle. He'd reconnected with his brothers and spent time with his niece and nephew. His stay in Portland had been productive.

He'd even fallen in love.

At least, he thought so. On his first free day at home, he prowled through his apartment and wondered how in blazes people knew when they were in love. How did one discern whether feelings were love or a powerful desire? Or need? Or infatuation?

Eden had made it clear that a temporary relationship could hurt her. He wouldn't hurt her for the world. He couldn't afford to make a mistake.

The first time she'd told him their relationship had to be nipped in the bud, he'd pretended to agree. His plan at that time had been to woo her, anyway. A man could woo without sex.

Probably.

The day of the commercial shoot, however, he'd heard her pain loud and clear. Someone or something—her stepfather, the situation with her mother, a former boyfriend?—had hurt her so badly that the next man who came into her life would have to stay. He'd have to know himself well enough to trust his own constancy. LJ didn't know if he could be that man. Eden had pointed out the truth: he'd never made a long-term commitment to anyone outside his immediate family.

Tired of aimlessly pacing and of thoughts that refused to culminate in a solution, he strode purposefully to the bookshelf to see if he could distract himself. Scanning almost every title in his collection, he rejected them all. Nothing was going to command his focus today, nothing but an answer to the riddle of romance in general and his relationship with Eden in particular. About to turn away, he paused as his gaze settled on the title, *The Most Important Thing*. His father's first book.

Pulling it from the shelf, he stared hard at the cover. He hadn't read the book in years, not since the first time, when it had made him feel inadequate.

You don't have the character to raise a family.

As if it were brand-new, the thought whomped him in the gut. His father had never said those words, not out loud; what he'd written, however, had plagued LJ quietly for years.

After the first read years ago, LJ had tried to laugh off his father's mandates about work and family and the values that made a man. LJ remembered saying to his friends, "Guess I'm a businessman through and through." He'd become aggressively single.

"I didn't want to fail in my father's eyes, so I decided not to try at all." He said the words with a kind of wonder, almost a compassion for the young man he now recognized as searching and scared and angry.

Perhaps Terrence, also a businessman at heart, had felt a similar shame and a similar need to disassociate from Lawrence Logan's powerful words.

LJ was sure his father had not meant to be judgmental, but such strong opinions tended to have strong effects.

Curious now, LJ carried the book to an armchair by the window, sat and opened it to the dedication page. "For my wife and children, the meaning of my life and the life of my days. You are my most important thing."

LJ believed that. Lawrence had never left any doubt about the dedication's sincerity. Waiting for the usual feeling of pressure, the burdensome sense of inadequacy he typically felt in the face of his father's family values, he was surprised and bemused to discover a much more mellow response. A kind of whispering envy.

Turning to the Table of Contents, he saw the chapter heading, *Putting Family First: Why and How.* Finding the first page of the chapter, he read the quote: "He who takes no risks, risks it all."

Understanding shot through LJ's body like a bolt of lightning as he read on. He didn't remember this chapter, didn't recall the genuine anxiety threading through his father's description of returning to college to study psychology while simultaneously trying to provide for a wife and four children. When LJ looked back at that time, he recalled two busy parents who had religiously set aside their evenings and weekends for child-centered activities. His father had studied late at night and early in the morning and always, always had joined his boys for breakfast. LJ knew for a fact that Lawrence had arisen before the sun was up to hit the books again.

As he read on he saw for the first time, and saw very clearly, that his father never had suggested eschewing career in favor of family; rather, he had cautioned against allowing the family to suffer for any reason.

"You will work twice as hard, and that's on an easy day. You will wonder how you can face another night of no sleep and still remember your name. Then small arms will encircle your neck. A stuffed animal hospital will be established in your living room, and you will be elected doctor.

"If courage and wisdom prevail, you'll realize that healing the teddy bear is your most important job to date. And you will rise once more, tired but willing, to meet the challenge."

LJ's eyes began to moisten. He remembered that teddy bear hospital, and for the first time he understood: Lawrence had been scared, too.

Closing his eyes, he held the book and allowed his new discovery to wash away the shame and guilt. Confusion was part of the package when you made the choice to love. A feeling of uncertainty didn't mean he'd be a rotten family man. It meant he'd fit right in with the legions of working parents around him.

LJ felt a weight lift off his chest. Another, however, settled on his shoulders. Deciding he wanted to be a family man was not his biggest hurdle. The family he wanted was still out of reach.

Opening his eyes, he carried the book to

his home office, where he sat behind the desk. He'd always had great inspiration here, solving problems that had continued to plague him at work. Hoping for inspiration now, he set the book on his blotter and picked up the phone. It was time for a long-overdue discussion with the man who'd brought him into the world and had been trying to teach him how to live it ever since. LJ knew he had resisted long enough. Wanting Eden made him humble. Was he selfless enough to be a good husband, a good father? Lawrence, Sr., would tell him straight out.

Wielding a meat cleaver, Eden chopped walnuts with staccato precision and far more force than necessary. She broke eggs into oil and sugar and whisked with the same excessive energy, pouring her frustration into banana bread batter.

"I can turn a blind eye to crimes against nut meats, but if you crack my favorite Pyrex bowl, I'll never forgive you." Liberty crossed the kitchen to grab a bottle of iced tea from the refrigerator.

Following the pattern she'd set over the past week, Eden did not look up. "It's almost impossible to crack Pyrex with a whisk," she muttered.

"In case you haven't noticed, I've been trying for days to find out what's wrong with you. If you want me to shut up and mind my own business, just say so. But please stop ignoring me."

Eden stiffened, well aware that she'd been withdrawn. She hadn't cooked a proper meal and barely had the energy or desire to drag herself to work, but she'd baked four batches of oatmeal cookies, two apricot-brandy bundt cakes, thirty-six mini carrot muffins and an apple pie. At first, she'd joked to herself that she must have bipolar baking disorder, but now the imbalance in her life didn't seem funny. Because the nights were filled with too many thoughts, she hadn't slept in days. Every morning she awoke jittery and restless, trying not to think about LJ and wondering if she'd made a huge mistake.

All her adult life she'd wondered if she had the potential to fall as far down the rabbit hole as her mother. If a few weeks of knowing LJ Logan could make her react this way, she figured she had her answer.

"I'm fine," she insisted to Liberty nonetheless, ill prepared to discuss feelings that frightened her so completely. Pulling a potato masher from a drawer, she began to squash a couple of innocent bananas.

"Okay, I'm outta here." Exasperated, Liberty grabbed an orange and headed out as the doorbell rang. "I'll get it," she called on her way into the living room.

The buzz of voices from the front of the house enervated Eden until it faded away. She reapplied herself to her baking, then startled when someone spoke from the doorway.

"I left four messages this week. You're not pickin' up, you're not returnin' calls. What's a mother got to do to talk to her only child?"

Feeling as if she moved in slow motion, Eden turned to find Gwen Carter standing in the doorway. "Mama?" she whispered.

Gwen took two steps into the kitchen and opened her arms. "I know when somethin's wrong with my girl. Liberty called—she's worried about you. Now get into these arms and tell me what's so awful that you can't pick up the phone."

Even as she meant to say, "Nothing's wrong. I'm fine", Eden found herself in her

mother's embrace, and all the tears she'd
been too frightened to cry before came
pouring out.

"Don't be mad at Liberty, darlin', she
cares too much not to interfere when you're
hurtin'." Gwen's southern lilt, which had
never flattened out as Eden's had, soothed
her daughter's jangled nerves.

With her hands wrapped around the mug
of tea her mother had made for her, Eden
murmured, "I'm sorry you had to come all
the way out here, Mama. I should have called
you back, but I—"

"Shh." Gwen placed her long artist's
fingers on Eden's arm. "You think I mind
mothering you? It's my privilege. When
Liberty called and told me she thought you
were feelin' bad about a man, I figured it
was time to have that talk we've always
avoided."

Eden didn't know whether to feel more
unsettled by the thought of Liberty reporting
to her mother or by the ominous way her
mother said "that talk."

"What talk, Mama?"

Gwen settled herself at the breakfast bar,

perching gracefully on the stool next to Eden's. With infinite love, she reached up to smooth the blond hair Eden had inherited from her.

"I remember the first time you fell in love. You'd gone away to college and planned to bring your beau home at Christmas. But you showed up by yourself and didn't say a word about what had happened. All through the holiday, you never shed a tear, not as far as I saw. You were eighteen, and I hadn't been a mother to you in so long, I didn't know what to do. So I stood back and watched." Eyes as blue as Eden's filled with regret. "I watched you ache and pretend you weren't hurt. And when you came home that summer, I knew you were runnin' around with too many boys, hopin' that would make the hurt go away. I wanted so badly to tell you not to be afraid."

Surprise and grief shot through Eden's chest. "You shouldn't feel guilty, Mama. You did fine."

Gwen shook her head vehemently. "I know how it was, Edie. I was there. We learn by example how to let ourselves feel." Taking her daughter's face between her hands, she made Eden look at her. "My depression made you afraid to be sad. Afraid to feel anything too strongly. I know that. I bet you're just petrified right now, 'cause Liberty says sparks were flyin' every which way the day she saw you with this beau of yours." Endless compassion filled Gwen's expression. "Don't be scared, baby. Feel everything. Love won't drive you crazy, but the fear of it might."

Pain shot through Eden like a lightning bolt dipped in fire. Her mother had hit so close to the truth, but her advice was no comfort. "Oh, Mama, how can you say that? Our lives were ruined when John left. Loving him did drive you—" She stopped abruptly.

"Crazy?" Gwen smiled. "Sugar, I was crazy long before John decided to leave. That's part of what drove us apart."

Eden jumped up from the table. "You were not crazy! Everything was fine until he bailed out."

"Darling, that's not true." Gwen reached for Eden's hand. "When I married John I was already having symptoms, but he and I both chose to ignore them. I suppose we hoped that if I had someone to distract me, I'd be fine."

"I don't remember anything being wrong with you," Eden insisted. "You were happy."

Gwen laughed. "To a child, I'm sure I seemed like a barrel of laughs in the early days. But John ran interference for me a lot as it got worse, sweet pea. I'd do something nutty, and he'd clean up the mess. He tried to protect you from it. At first I appreciated his efforts. But then…" She shrugged. "I wound up feeling controlled and smothered. I began to hate him for his help. He wound up resentful and, I'm sure, exhausted, and in any case, you can't wish mental illness away. I told him to leave, sugar. You've got to understand that. John didn't abandon us. I ordered him out."

The pain in Eden's chest turned into a deep burn. That wasn't how she remembered it. Confusion added to her frustration. "Why do you excuse him, Mama? Whatever happened, he promised to love you in sickness and in health and then he never showed his face again." Tears filled her until she honestly thought she might choke on them.

This was why she never spoke about John, tried not even to think about him. He hadn't married only her mother. Eden had stood between John and Gwen the day they had wed. On a silky white runner, the three of them had held hands. Eden had said, "I do," and though she hadn't understood all the vows, she had known they had something to do with love and something to do with forever.

Ten years old when her mother and John divorced, she didn't remember all the details, but in unguarded moments the feelings tried to knock her around as if John had sat her down and told her he was leaving just yesterday. Anger filled every cell.

"John lied, Mama. He told me he was going away for a while and then he'd see us again. But he left and never looked back, and if he had maybe..." She choked up, unable to finish.

Tears filled Gwen's eyes, too, but her sorrow was for the little girl who had decided that love was as cozy as an atomic bomb. Summoning the resolve she'd acquired over the years, Gwen completed Eden's sentence without a whisper of self-pity. "If John had come back, then maybe I wouldn't have gone from 'fun' to 'certifiable'?" Standing, she took Eden's hands. "The man Liberty told me about, Edie…do you love him?"

"Mama, please, let's not—"

"Eden Carter, I asked you an important question, and I expect an honest answer. Do you love him?"

Looking away, Eden mumbled, "I think so."

Gwen squeezed her hands. "Don't think. Just answer the question."

The command was strikingly similar to LJ's comment that she thought too much. Steeling herself against a deluge of feeling, Eden admitted, "When we're with him—Liam and I—everything seems… right. I forget to be careful with myself. My heart forgets everything." She shook her head. "That sounds so—"

"Stop right there." Keeping hold of Eden's hands, Gwen tugged her down to the chair and leaned forward. "Listen carefully. I knew already in my teens that I had an illness. I didn't know what it was, and I certainly didn't know how to get help, so I pretended everyone else was crazy and I was perfectly fine. Just less inhibited. When you were in your teens and taking care of me, I was petrified you'd be sick, too. I watched you like a hawk, baby. I worried myself sick." Her lips curved with irony. "Make that 'sicker.'"

Eden's heart pounded in her throat. "I never knew that. You never suggested—"

"Well, of course not! You were so responsible, so serious. You didn't need another burden. But, Edie, hear me on this, sugar—you're fine. *Fine.* There is nothin' wrong with you that a little courage won't fix. All you need is less fear and more faith that people can come and go and you'll be all right. Hearts are strongest after they're broken and healed. Yours included."

Tears began to roll down Eden's cheeks. Gwen had named the secret dread Eden had lived with for over two decades—that enough grief might awaken in her a depression akin to her mother's. She'd been afraid to grieve when John left. It had felt safer to get angry.

"Forgive me, Edie. It's time."

"What?" Eden gazed at her mother, honestly baffled by the comment. "I don't blame you for anything."

"Forgive me for what my illness took from you. Forgive life for giving us the struggles we faced. And don't say you've already done it, because if that were true, I'd be meeting this new man of yours." Bringing her daughter's hands toward her lips, she gave them a kiss. "Let go. It's time, baby. Nothing in this world has to be perfect to be beautiful—not a body, not a mind and definitely not a relationship."

Eden had worked so hard not to be like Gwen. Now that seemed almost shamefully churlish. Sitting before her was a woman whose very brokenness had led her to become beautifully, admirably whole.

She looked, really looked at her mother. "Do you think you'll ever fall in love again, Mama?"

Gwen's beautiful face turned still lovelier as her expression grew almost mischievous. "I am in love. With my friends. With my work. With you and Liam and with the gal in the mirror. I've fallen in love with life on life's terms, sugar, and if that includes a new man, which it has once or twice—" she winked "—then I'll hop on that ride again, too. The important thing isn't that others don't abandon us, Edie, it's that we learn not to abandon ourselves."

When Gwen enfolded her daughter in her arms, Eden felt her mother's confidence. She'd believed adoring Liam taught her everything she needed to know about love, but today she understood that the real work of loving unconditionally was about to begin.

"How long are you staying, Mama?" she asked as she laid her head against a shoulder that was broader than it looked.

Gwen pressed her lips to the top of Eden's head and murmured, "As long as it takes, sugar. I'll be with you as long as it takes."

Chapter Fifteen

When Eden walked into the same house in which they'd shot the commercial for the Children's Connection, she felt like a celebrity walking into a movie premiere. If the house had been beautiful before, it was positively exquisite now, dressed to the nines with flowers, candles and long tables displaying an elegant array of hors d'oeuvres and sweets.

Her mother had returned to New Mexico with a promise from Eden to bring Liam out there for Christmas. During her visit, she and Eden had talked quite a bit about the past, comparing memories, crying together and laughing more about the difficult times than Eden had imagined possible. When Eden drove Gwen to the airport, she felt lighter and stronger, as if she'd lost unnecessary flab but gained bone and muscle.

The invitation to tonight's screening of the commercial had brought with it a rush of feeling for LJ, not that she'd ever stopped thinking about him.

He hadn't contacted her, nor had she attempted to get in touch with him. They'd already danced an emotional cha-cha with her stepping back more than she should have. It wouldn't have been fair to him to get in touch before she was sure—not about him, but about herself.

Smoothing the skirt of her red dress, she moved from foyer to living room, waving when she saw Stacey Logan heading toward her with a flute of champagne.

"Is alcohol still off-limits for you?" Stacey greeted her by asking with a grin. "Because if you're not breastfeeding, this stuff is yummy."

Eden laughed. "I can probably afford a few sips. Liam is pretty enamored of strained bananas and whole wheat crackers these days."

They found a strolling waiter and scored a glass for Eden. Stacey raised her flute for a toast. "To your television debut. I hear the commercial is great. And it's a good thing, too." She lowered her voice, her gaze turning worried. "Have you heard the latest?"

"I don't know. Latest about…?"

"More bad news for Terrence and Leslie. For the clinic in general, I suppose. Robbie has disappeared. Nancy hasn't seen or heard from him in days. She's beside herself."

Eden's stomach clenched in an awful sympathy. "But why? Not because of the bad press?"

Stacey stared down at her champagne. "I think so. Can you imagine? Some so-called journalist does a hatchet job on your husband, and he's so riddled with guilt he thinks the only answer is to leave everything he loves? I'd want to rip the reporter's heart out." She looked up and grimaced. "Sorry."

Eden shook her head. "Don't be. I'd feel the same. If someone hurt—"

She stopped herself. In truth, the person who had most recently hurt LJ was her.

Stacey glanced at her quizzically, but didn't press her to complete the sentence.

"They're planning to air the commercial throughout the Pacific Northwest, you know."

"No, I didn't know. Who told you?"

"Terrence had to approve the final product and told LJ he was thrilled. LJ told Jake."

Eden's heart behaved as if she'd downed a triple-shot latte. It was all she could do not to look wildly around the room until Stacey added, "Jake and LJ have been in touch quite a bit." She lowered her voice. "They're scheming ways to get their dad to try again to reconcile with Terrence."

"Oh. So they've been talking on the phone, you mean?"

"Yes. Apparently, LJ reread Lawrence's book and called his dad to talk about it. He actually told Lawrence to reread what he'd written and then phone Terrence. Pretty nervy. Doctor, heal thyself." She chuckled. "Jake, Ryan and Scott said they're going to divvy up LJ's share of the inheritance."

"Was his father that angry?"

"No. More taken aback, I think. He told LJ it wasn't any of the boys' business. Of course, as soon as LJ shared that piece of information with his alpha-male brothers, they made it their mission to butt in until the cold war is over."

Eden took a slow sip of champagne. Family values. How she'd misjudged the good man she'd fallen for. Caring and loyalty were part of his nature. What if something happened to him the way it had to Robbie Logan? She would want to be there. She would want the *right* to be there.

"Do you think LJ will come back to Portland anytime soon?"

She'd been wondering if LJ had told anyone what had gone on between the two of them. Stacey's understanding expression gave her the answer.

"It's none of my business, of course," the other woman said, "but I have some experience with relationships that lose their way. I hope you won't give up if you still feel something. For some reason these Logan men seem to take a long time to come to their senses where women are concerned. Once they do, though, it's worth the wait. I can vouch for that."

"Thanks, Stacey. In this case, though, I'm the one who needed to come to her senses."

"Really?" Stacey sipped her champagne.

"Gorgeous house, isn't it? Fabulous neighborhood, too. Do you know some of the best elementary schools in Oregon are in this district?"

"No, I didn't know."

"It's for sale, you know. I wonder if Jake has his checkbook with him?" She smiled. "Let's go explore. I don't think they're going to screen the commercial for a while yet. Everyone's still eating."

Stacey strolled toward the garden with Eden trailing behind. She wanted to ask Stacey a million and one questions about LJ, beginning with where was he right now. It took a Herculean effort to focus on the here and now. She certainly didn't want to make Stacey uncomfortable.

"Even the yard is huge," Stacey exclaimed, leading Eden along a series of stone pathways. "I think there's a gazebo around here somewhere."

Lights at ground level illuminated the walkways.

"Stacey!" Eden caught up as her friend reached for the latch of a tall gate. "Look." She nodded to a rectangular white sign that read This Area Reserved for Private Party.

Stacey studied the note briefly then said, "Not a problem. It must mean it's reserved for our party." Before Eden could suggest otherwise, she pushed the gate open.

Eden almost didn't recognize the patio where LJ had given her the massage, and where they had had their last conversation, the one she wished she could do over. The meditative oasis had been turned into a sultry, private nook with lanterns hung from branches and perched along the stone fence. Gorgeous gold linen draped a table for two.

"We'd better go," Eden whispered, plucking at Stacey's gauzy sleeve. "This really does look private."

"Yeah," she said. Grabbing Eden's arm, she hustled them both behind a large rhododendron. "Let's watch."

"Stacey!" Eden resisted, peering through the broad leaves and fluffy flowers. "This isn't right. We can't spy on—"

"Shh. Sure we can. Think of it as reality TV."

Even without knowing LJ's sister-in-law well, Eden was sure she'd temporarily lost a screw. When she heard footsteps heading their way from the other side of the patio, however, she hopped quickly behind the plant.

"Good girl," Stacey whispered. "He who hesitates is lost."

Eden only hoped she could explain this aberrant behavior to Terrence, should her boss hear that she'd been spying on people at a company-hosted party. She looked around for a way to escape when two waiters dressed in black pants and neon-white shirts entered the patio to add flowers and candles to the table.

They continued to place and light candles until the patio glowed as if dozens of tiny moons lit the sky from below.

The waiters left, and a tall tuxedoed gentleman took their place. Standing by the table, he checked to make sure everything was the way he'd requested it, then checked his watch. He looked excited and nervous.

"Now it's getting interesting," Stacey whispered. "Do you still want to leave?"

Unable to speak and knowing Stacey didn't require an answer anyway, Eden merely shook her head.

"Well, I think I'll go. I want to find Jake, grab a little something to eat. I'm famished."

Squeezing between Eden and the stone wall surrounding the private patio, Stacey emerged from the bushes and checked her clothing for stray leaves.

"Hi." She waved to LJ. Jerking a thumb, she indicated the rhododendron. "Your date's in there. Your move."

LJ frowned. "I asked you to get her out to the patio, not hide her in the bushes." He strode to the location his sister-in-law indicated.

"I know. I added that part myself. I'm practicing spontaneity and creativity." She patted LJ's upper arm. "Good luck. Don't blow it."

"Thanks for the support."

With a last grin at Eden's hiding place, Stacey exited the small garden patio.

LJ parted some branches and peeked in. "Hi."

"Hello." His eyes glowed warmer than the candles, yet she shivered. "I didn't expect to see you tonight."

"This isn't exactly how I planned it. Can you come out of there? I didn't want to scare you into hiding."

Eden edged along the wall until she emerged from the rhododendrons and self-consciously brushed at her hair. "I'm not scared."

"You look beautiful."

"So do you—handsome, I mean."

LJ sighed as a protracted moment passed. "I planned this whole evening. Ten minutes ago I knew exactly what I wanted to say. Now I can't think of a thing."

"There is a lot to talk about," she agreed.

"Yeah. Give me a minute just to look at you again, and I'll remember everything."

"Okay, I'll give you a minute. And while you're thinking…"

In her heels she only had to rise a tiny bit to reach his lips. She curved her arms around his neck. LJ inched back in surprise, then settled into the kiss like a man who'd been given back his life. Eden understood the feeling, smiling against him when he pulled her as close as he could.

"Please tell me that kiss means 'I'm glad you're back, don't ever leave,'" LJ begged when they parted. His fingers delving lovingly through her hair, he shook his head. "I missed you, Eden Carter. I missed your son. I can't love you for just a while and then turn it all off."

"Love?" Her heart wrapped itself around the word.

"Love. I know it's too soon. You're still right about my lousy track record with women. I'm asking you to trust me, anyway. I *need* you to trust me. Because more than anything in my life, I want my relationship with you and Liam to work."

"I have a lousy track record myself."

Her heart fluttered as if it wanted to take flight. She was perfectly content to stay in his arms for the remainder of the conversation, perfectly content even to postpone the conversation and get back to kissing, but he set her gently away from him.

"There are challenges," he admitted, looking serious. "I'm not denying that, but we can overcome anything we have to. I've been thinking about it, Eden. I've done nothing but think about it since I left." He guided her to the bench they'd sat on weeks before. "Sit here. I'm going to present this so logically, all your doubts will fade away."

Sweet humor replaced the last vestige of grief she'd felt since he'd gone. The intensity and passion in his eyes underscored his words. It was more than Eden had dared hope for, especially after chasing him away.

Doubts?

Lawrence Logan, Jr. had grace and elegance, integrity and warmth. He was charming with the public, genuine with her. He held something of himself back, a corner of his heart he gave to only a few. She felt certain now, after hours and hours of soul-searching, that she could take very good care of that heart.

"LJ," she whispered, ready to tell him she was all done with doubts, that they'd been mostly about herself, anyway, but he had more to say and rushed on.

"Here." Leaving her briefly, he poured a glass of champagne from the silver bucket near the table, returned to hand it to her. Then he began to pace as if making a presentation to a board of directors. "All right, here we go—the reasons why obstacles don't mean anything. I'm going to address your concerns one by one. First, there's the geographical issue. You're in Oregon, I'm in New York. But that's not going to be a problem."

"It isn't?" Feeling almost giddy, she took a sip of the delicious champagne. "I'm all ears."

"Good. The way I've figured it, my business can be moved gradually over the course of this year. By January I can be settled in Portland. In the meantime I'll fly back regularly. You're probably wondering now how we can get to know each other in a profound way with all this travel early in our relationship."

"Hmm." Eden's stomach growled. She felt hungry for the first time in two weeks. "That is a good point."

"And it's understandable that you want to be cautious about a long-distance relationship. I'd be resistant, too, in your situation. I don't want you traveling back and forth with Liam."

Setting her champagne flute beside her on the stone bench, she shook her head. "Uh-oh. I think we do have a problem here."

LJ's handsome jaw set firmly. "No, we don't. Believe me, Eden, I've been eating, breathing and dreaming about us. I've anticipated every obstacle and brainstormed a way around, over or through them all."

"And I really, truly appreciate it. I think there's one thing, though, that you were not able to anticipate." Reaching for her shoulder bag, she opened it to withdraw an envelope.

LJ's expression darkened considerably when he recognized what she held. "Plane tickets?"

"Plane tickets," she confirmed. "I've been thinking a lot, too." She ran her fingertips thoughtfully along the top edge of the envelope. "My turn to talk, okay?"

After a solemn nod from LJ, she continued. "My mother was just here in Portland. She stayed a week, and we had lots of difficult, wonderful talks. The kind you can only have with the people who know your history. I decided family is the most important thing in the world to me and that my family is larger than only Liam and me." Looking as deeply into his eyes as she could, she admitted, "I've tried and tried to avoid the things I can't control—like any person who could possibly get close enough to hurt me—but now I know that I want Thanksgivings with more people than chairs, and Christmases with way too many presents and Easters with arguments about who ate whose chocolate bunny. I want regular boring weekends with everyone disagreeing about which movie to rent." She held up the tickets. "So I bought these."

"You're going to New Mexico," he said flatly, "to be near your mother."

"I'd like to be near my mom, yes, but I

tend to burn in hot southern climates. So, no, I'm not going to go to New Mexico, not to stay. I bought tickets for somewhere with more of a winter. And fall. And spring. I love spring. Being in love in the spring would be marvelous."

"What are you saying? You're planning to leave Oregon permanently? Oregon has a spring."

It was mean to tease him, but he looked adorable when he was disgruntled. "Nope," she said equally, "I have no plans—yet—to move permanently. And, yes, Oregon does have a spring. And a perfect green summer and a golden fall and a wet, sludgy winter that I love." She moved closer, the plane tickets in her hands. "What Oregon doesn't have—" she took the tickets from their folder and held them for LJ to see "—is you."

He squinted, touched the evidence. "New York. It's a round-trip to New York."

"I have your home phone number in here, too." She patted the red, quilted purse slung over her shoulder. "I hadn't decided yet whether to call before we left or after. I didn't want you to tell me not to come. I had this fantasy of just showing up on your doorstep.

But then I realized you might not have a doorstep. You might live in one of those buildings where they have to buzz you up. I could be standing outside a mighty long time with a baby in a sling and egg all over my face—"

She stopped when he swept her close then cradled her cheeks with his hands. "Such a beautiful face." He kissed her long and hard. "You were coming to see me?" he confirmed when the kiss ended. "I'm not just dreaming this, right?"

Eden leaned into him, looking up. "If you are, don't worry. We're having the same dream. I knew right away that you were part of my fantasy, the white knight who rides in on his charger, then takes off his armor and fixes his kid's bike." She shook her head. "That's an awful lot of pressure and expectation to put on anyone, though."

"Do you hear me complaining? For the first time in my life, I *want* to be someone's white knight. Yours and Liam's. I think about you two, and I know I want to be there for anything life throws our way."

Taking his hands in hers, she gave them a squeeze and held them close to her heart. "I have a lot to tell you. I mean, truly a lot. You need to know about my mom and how bad it got when she had her breakdown. Conditions like hers can run in a family, and you have to consider that. Because even if it skipped a generation with me, it could be an issue in the future…if we stay together, I mean, and if we have a child. And there's Liam's future to consider. I'll always be there for him, of course, but if—"

Bending forward, he gave her a strong, swift kiss. "You say 'if' way too much. We're going to have plenty of time to get know each other—you, me and Liam. So when we get married—*when* not *if*—you'll know that I mean 'for better or worse' no matter what. Any child we add to the family will have all our love and support, too. Plus open lines of communication, always. I figure a kid could do a lot worse."

LJ's strength, his commitment, acted like sun on snow, melting the worries Eden had carried alone for too long. Hope bloomed like spring in her heart as, for the first time in her adult life, happily-ever-after stood close enough to touch.

Dreamy and excited and sure, she leaned

into LJ, unable to summon a lick of fear even when he said, "We may have a more immediate problem, though."

"What's that?"

"Well, I've been thinking we'd do most of our courting on the West Coast."

"Courting?" Nodding, Eden grinned. "I like that."

"Good. Do you like the idea of my moving to Portland?"

She blinked in surprise. "Well, sure. But really, your business—"

"Can be moved or can function on both coasts. I like Portland, Eden. Liam will have grandparents and cousins here, and housing shouldn't be a problem. I've kind of, sort of—well, definitely—found something."

Eden pulled away to look at him. He gazed back with an eyebrow raised in question. "Kind of, sort of definitely? Don't stop now, you're on a roll."

Taking his arms from around her waist, he settled his hands on her shoulders and frowned into her eyes. "I've either made a huge mistake in our relationship or you will remember this as one of the most romantic gestures I will ever make."

Her eyes widened. "Nice build-up of anticipation. Go on."

LJ took a steadying breath. "When we first sat on that bench—" he nodded to the one behind her "—during the commercial shoot, and I was rubbing your shoulders, I thought, 'This is it. This is where I want to be forty years from now—standing behind this bench, rubbing this woman's shoulders and feeling her relax.'"

Wordlessly Eden reached up to put her hands atop his.

"One of the reasons we've had liberal use of this place," he continued, "is that the owners retired to Hawaii. So when I saw the house originally, it was for sale, lock, stock and barrel." He stopped there, waiting.

Eden stared, mouth agape. "You didn't."

"Only earnest money," he hastened to assure her. "If you hate the idea, dislike anything about the place...or if you love the house, hate the decor, whatever, we can deal with it. We can even forget the whole thing and look for something else together. I'm not marrying a house, so don't be afraid to say, 'Junior, what the hell were you thinking?'" He shook his head when she remained silently shocked. "Oh, boy. This is bad, isn't it? Stacey warned me women like to decorate their own homes."

"I've watched exactly one half of one episode of HGTV," she croaked when she could make a sound, "and only because two of Liberty's friends were on *House Hunters*. And you told me not to call you Junior."

"You can call me anything you want. Just tell me what you think."

"I love this place."

"Still—"

It was no hardship to Eden to silence LJ's doubts. "I don't *need* a house like this. We can do our courting—" she grinned again, loving the concept "—anywhere. But, yes, Lawrence Logan, I will remember your buying our bench—and the house that goes with it—as one of the most romantic gestures ever."

LJ let his arms slide down so that he was resting his hands on the small of her back. He allowed a long, deep sigh of pure relief. "All right, I say we keep it then. Less time spent house hunting and decorating means more time spent kissing. Not that that was my motive."

"Of course not."

They got a brief head start on the kissing nonetheless and then LJ said, "What do you say we blow this shindig and head to your place?"

"What about screening the commercial?"

"I set that up for the staff, but we could have watched it at the Children's Connection. The party was strictly a ruse to get you here."

"A ruse? You mean you manipulated all these poor people?"

"Yes, but the food's good."

"That's true."

"Let's go. Besides, I miss the little guy."

"An evening with family," Eden said. "That sounds just right." They smiled into each other's eyes. Stepping away, LJ grabbed her hand and walked her to the gate. It was the first time they'd walked hand in hand. Amazing that such simple contact could feel positively thrilling.

"We should tell someone we're leaving," she said reluctantly.

"Nooo," LJ groaned. "We'll never get out of here. Jake and Stacey know what I was up to tonight. They'll be like bloodhounds searching for information to share with the rest of the family."

Holding firm at the gate, Eden asked, "Does Jake carry a cell phone?"

"Sure. He's a doctor. He probably won't answer, but he checks his messages every fifteen minutes. It's annoying as hell. Stacey's trying to break him of it."

Eden pulled her phone from her purse. "What's his number?" Dialing as LJ spoke, she held the tiny cell phone to her ear. "Jake," she said when she got his voice mail, "this is Eden Carter. I'm calling to let you know that I'm taking your brother captive for the rest of the night. Please tell Stacey I'm going to plant rhododendron all around the house and that she's welcome to hide in them anytime. And ask her how she feels about wearing pink."

Grinning up at LJ, her heart brimming with confidence, Eden concluded, "I want my bridesmaids to wear pink."

LJ reached for the phone. "Did you copy that, bro? I'm getting married. You're going to be an uncle."

As if they'd been a couple for years, LJ and Eden simultaneously reached for each other's hands.

"I'm going to be a dad," he added with

quiet awe and a goofy smile. "I have only one more thing to say before my bride-to-be and I blow this joint. Remember when you told me falling in love is like seeing the ocean for the first time—bigger and more amazing than anything you've seen before? Well, you can tell Scott and Ryan for me that their brother Jake is a wise man. I just jumped in, and the water's great."

* * * * *

Look for ONE MAN'S FAMILY
by Brenda Harlen
the fifth book in the new Special Edition
continuity
LOGAN'S LEGACY REVISITED
On sale May 2007,
wherever Silhouette Books are sold.

Dante Raintree stood with his arms crossed as he watched the woman on the monitor. The image was in black and white to better show details; color distracted the brain. He focused on her hands, watching every move she made, but what struck him most was how uncommonly *still* she was. She didn't fidget or play with her chips, or look around at the other players. She peeked once at her down card, then didn't touch it again, signaling for another hit by tapping a fingernail on the table. Just because she didn't seem to be paying attention to the other players, though, didn't mean she was as unaware as she seemed.

"What's her name?" Dante asked.

"Lorna Clay," replied his chief of security, Al Rayburn.

"At first I thought she was counting, but she doesn't pay enough attention."

"She's paying attention, all right," Dante murmured. "You just don't see her doing it." A card counter had to remember every card played. Supposedly counting cards was impossible with the number of decks used by the casinos, but there were those rare individuals who could calculate the odds even with multiple decks.

"I thought that, too," said Al. "But look at this piece of tape coming up. Someone she knows comes up to her and speaks, she looks around and starts chatting, completely misses the play of the people to her left—and doesn't look around even when the deal comes back to her, just taps that finger. And damn if she didn't win. Again."

Dante watched the tape, rewound it, watched it again. Then he watched it a third time. There had to be something he was missing, because he couldn't pick out a single giveaway.

"If she's cheating," Al said with something like respect, "she's the best I've ever seen."

"What does your gut say?"

Al scratched the side of his jaw, considering. Finally, he said, "If she isn't cheating, she's the luckiest person walking. She wins. Week in, week out, she wins. Never a huge amount, but I ran the numbers and she's into us for about five grand a week. Hell, boss, on her way out of the casino she'll stop by a slot machine, feed a dollar in and walk away with at least fifty. It's never the same machine, either. I've had her watched, I've had her followed, I've even looked for the same faces in the casino every time she's in here, and I can't find a common denominator."

"Is she here now?"

"She came in about half an hour ago. She's playing blackjack, as usual."

"Bring her to my office," Dante said, making a swift decision. "Don't make a scene."

"Got it," said Al, turning on his heel and leaving the security center.

Dante left, too, going up to his office. His face was calm. Normally he would leave it to Al to deal with a cheater, but he was curious. How was she doing it? There were a lot of bad cheaters, a few good ones, and every so often one would come along who was the stuff of which legends were made: the cheater who didn't get caught, even when people were alert and the camera was on him—or, in this case, her.

It was possible to simply be lucky, as most people understood luck. Chance could turn a habitual loser into a big-time winner. Casinos, in fact, thrived on that hope. But luck itself wasn't habitual, and he knew that what passed for luck was often something else: cheating. And there was the other kind of luck, the kind he himself possessed, but it depended not on chance but on who and what he was. He knew it was an innate power and not Dame Fortune's erratic smile. Since power like his was rare, the odds made it likely the woman he'd been watching was merely a very clever cheat.

Her skill could provide her with a very good living, he thought, doing some swift calculations in his head. Five grand a week equaled $260,000 a year, and that was just from his casino. She probably hit them all, careful to keep the numbers relatively low so she stayed under the radar.

He wondered how long she'd been taking him, how long she'd been winning a little here, a little there, before Al noticed.

The curtains were open on the wall-to-wall window in his office, giving the impression, when one first opened the door, of stepping out onto a covered balcony. The glazed window faced west, so he could catch the sunsets. The sun was low now, the sky painted in purple and gold. At his home in the mountains, most of the windows faced east, affording him views of the sunrise. Something in him needed both the greeting and the goodbye of the sun. He'd always been drawn to sunlight, maybe because fire was his element to call, to control.

He checked his internal time: four minutes until sundown. Without checking the sunrise tables every day, he knew exactly when the sun would slide behind the mountains. He didn't own an alarm clock. He didn't need one. He was so acutely attuned to the sun's position that he had only to check within himself to know the time. As for waking at a particular time, he was one of those people who could tell himself to wake at a certain time, and he did. That talent had nothing to do with being Raintree, so he didn't have to hide it; a lot of perfectly ordinary people had the same ability.

He had other talents and abilities, however, that did require careful shielding. The long days of summer instilled in him an almost sexual high, when he could feel contained power buzzing just beneath his skin. He had to be doubly careful not to cause candles to leap into flame just by his presence, or to start wildfires with a glance in the dry-as-tinder brush. He loved Reno; he didn't want to burn it down. He just felt so damn *alive* with all the sunshine pouring down that he wanted to let the energy pour through him instead of holding it inside.

This must be how his brother Gideon felt while pulling lightning, all that hot power searing through his muscles, his veins. They had this in common, the connection with raw power. All the members of the far-flung Raintree clan had some power, some heightened ability, but only members of the royal family could channel and control the earth's natural energies.

Dante wasn't just of the royal family, he was the Dranir, the leader of the entire clan. "Dranir" was synonymous with king, but the position he held wasn't ceremonial, it was one of sheer power. He was the oldest son of the previous Dranir, but he would have been passed over for the position if he hadn't also inherited the power to hold it.

Behind him came Al's distinctive knock on the door. The outer office was empty, Dante's secretary having gone home hours before. "Come in," he called, not turning from his view of the sunset.

The door opened, and Al said, "Mr. Raintree, this is Lorna Clay."

Dante turned and looked at the woman, all his senses on alert. The first thing he noticed was the vibrant color of her hair, a rich, dark red that encompassed a multitude of shades from copper to burgundy. The warm amber light danced along the iridescent strands, and he felt a hard tug of sheer lust in his gut. Looking at her hair was almost like looking at fire, and he had the same reaction.

The second thing he noticed was that she was spitting mad.

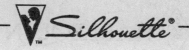

Silhouette SPECIAL EDITION™

Emotional, compelling stories that capture the intensity of living, loving and creating a family in today's world.

Silhouette Desire

Modern, passionate reads that are powerful and provocative.

Silhouette nocturne

Dramatic and sensual tales of paranormal romance.

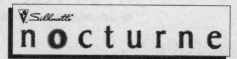

Silhouette Romantic SUSPENSE

Romances that are sparked by danger and fueled by passion.

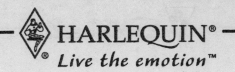

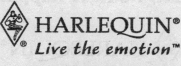

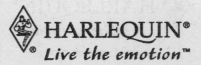

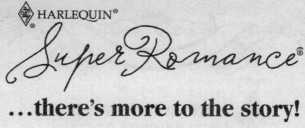
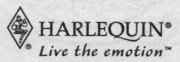

Harlequin® Historical
Historical Romantic Adventure!

Imagine a time of chivalrous knights and unconventional ladies, roguish rakes and impetuous heiresses, rugged cowboys and spirited frontierswomen—these rich and vivid tales will capture your imagination!

Harlequin Historical . . . they're too good to miss!